"What the hell are you doing, Garrett?"

"Kissing you, Jules." He grinned at her. "Pucker up, princess."

Amusement pulled her lips upward. "You are ridiculous."

Garrett lifted his hand to her cheek, his thumb brushing over her cheekbone. "Let me show you just how much chemistry is arcing between us."

When he heard her shaky breath, he knew she was as turned on as he was.

"Can I kiss you, Juliana?" he murmured.

Her "yes" was shaky but there, so he placed light kisses on her mouth, her jawline and her neck as his hand slid over her hip. He came back to her lips. When her mouth parted and the hand on the back of his neck tightened, he slid his tongue between her teeth.

* * *

Lost and Found Heir by Joss Wood is part of the Dynasties: DNA Dilemma series.

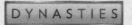

Will the results of one DNA test upend everything for this American blueblood family?
Don't miss a single twist or turn!

Secrets of a Bad Reputation
Wrong Brother, Right Kiss
Lost and Found Heir
The Secret Heir Returns

Dear Reader,

Welcome back to Portland, Maine, and book three of the Dynasties: DNA Dilemma series!

When Callum, the Ryder-White patriarch, suffers a heart attack, James Ryder-White takes the opportunity to make some life-changing decisions for himself, his family and for the son he has never acknowledged!

Despite his mother's refusal to discuss his parentage, Garrett Kaye has always believed Callum is his father, so it's a huge shock when he is proven wrong! Needing to get out of Portland, Maine, to have time to think about James's incredible offer and what it means for his future, he agrees to accompany the very lovely Jules Carson out of state.

Jules is a mixologist and does promotional pop-up bars. When she finds out that her second mom's boutique gin company is in desperate financial straits, she asks the very sexy Garrett to accompany her to Kate's ranch to try to discover a way to save her company. But in Colorado, learning about each other, they also learn more about themselves. And they might just find the love they both desperately need!

Happy reading!

Joss

Connect with me on:
Facebook: JossWoodAuthor
Twitter: JossWoodbooks
Bookbub: joss-wood
www.JossWoodBooks.com

JOSS WOOD

LOST AND FOUND HEIR

HARLEQUIN®
DESIRE™

Recycling programs
for this product may
not exist in your area.

ISBN-13: 978-1-335-73559-1

Lost and Found Heir

Copyright © 2022 by Joss Wood

For questions and comments about the quality of this book, please contact us at CustomerService@Harlequin.com.

Harlequin Enterprises ULC
22 Adelaide St. West, 41st Floor
Toronto, Ontario M5H 4E3, Canada
www.Harlequin.com

Printed in U.S.A.

Joss Wood loves books, coffee and traveling—especially to the wild places of southern Africa and, well, anywhere. She's a wife and a mom to two young adults. She's also a slave to two cats and a dog the size of a small cow. After a career in local economic development and business, Joss writes full-time from her home in KwaZulu-Natal, South Africa.

Books by Joss Wood

Harlequin Desire

Dynasties: DNA Dilemma

Secrets of a Bad Reputation
Wrong Brother, Right Kiss
Lost and Found Heir

Murphy International

One Little Indiscretion
Temptation at His Door
Back in His Ex's Bed

Harlequin Presents

South Africa's Scandalous Billionaires

How to Undo the Proud Billionaire
How to Win the Wild Billionaire

Visit her Author Profile page at Harlequin.com, or josswoodbooks.com, for more titles.

You can also find Joss Wood on Facebook, along with other Harlequin Desire authors, at Facebook.com/harlequindesireauthors!

One

Garrett Kaye wasn't having fun—he didn't know if he'd recognize fun if it bit him in the ass—but he was less bored than usual.

And that had to be a win.

He was at Ryder International's Annual Valentine's Day Ball seated at an exquisitely decorated table. The monotony of the black, white and silver theme—the ceiling was covered in a shimmery silver fabric interspersed with fairy lights, and the round tables were covered in an expensive white fabric printed with black roses—was broken by three-foot-high wineglasses standing in the center of the table, the bowls holding deep pink, red and white tulips and pops of bright greenery. The dinnerware was pure white, the cutlery a heavy silver, and the wine and champagne glasses were crystal.

The food, produced by a James Beard award–winning chef, was Michelin-star standard, the champagne was ridiculously tart and ludicrously expensive, and judging by the *ooh*s he'd heard, the swag bags were impressive. The smiles on the faces of his fellow guests told him that everyone was having a decent time. They should be, since they'd paid upward of one hundred thousand dollars for a ticket. Though, to be fair, for most of the guests, Garrett included, dropping so much money wasn't a problem.

Would he be here if it was anyone other than the Ryder-White clan hosting the ball? Probably not. To the members of that illustrious family, he was simply the son of Callum Ryder-White's assistant, a local boy and an international success story.

Yet, Callum and clan had no idea that with no effort at all, Garrett could tip over their carefully constructed applecarts.

"My first job was in Panama City, doing a gin promotion on the beach…"

At the sound of the melodious voice, Garrett pulled his attention back to the conversation at the table, where Jules Carlson—she of the abundant curls, warm brown skin and rocking body—was holding court. Her hazel eyes, a complex combination of green, gold and brown, fascinated him. When she looked or spoke to someone she liked, they sparked with warm gold flecks. When she laughed, those flecks turned to copper. Occasionally, he saw green-colored flames, but only when she spoke to him. He seemed to annoy her, and the thought amused him.

Hers was an abnormal reaction and one that piqued his interest.

Garrett knew he was a good-looking guy. That was fact, not ego. He was tall—at six-four, some would say too tall—and he kept his body fit and muscled. He was also a realist and knew that, thanks to his fat bank accounts, women would always treat him like he was a combination of a bachelor prince, bad-boy rock star and Mr. Universe.

Money, he knew, could whitewash everything.

But Jules Carlson—a world-famous mixologist and bartender—was comprehensively unimpressed by him. Interesting.

He liked interesting.

Garrett leaned back in his seat and undid the single button holding his tuxedo jacket closed, listening as Jules regaled the table with a story of one of her first pop-up bars where everything seemed to go wrong. She'd dropped a bottle of tequila on her foot but carried on working with a broken toe, a fight broke out, and she had a clothing malfunction: her bikini top slipped sideways, showing the customers more of her breast than she intended.

She had lovely breasts, Garrett decided, as his eyes skimmed her narrow frame. She was tall and slim with great curves. Curves her dress—a bold tangerine skirt and top comprising laser-cut geometric shapes in white, orange, gold and black baring patches of her torso, leaving much of that golden-brown skin uncovered—showed off to perfection. With its beaded spirals and shapes, the dress was a nod to her distant African ancestry. It was bold and sensuous and stood out in the sea of understated, mostly monochromatic dresses in the room.

"That pop-up bar was sponsored by Crazy Kate's Gin, wasn't it?" Tinsley Ryder-White asked, a tiny frown marring her pretty face. Like him, Tinsley had dark brown hair and blue eyes and the same angular face. It wasn't surprising that they looked a little alike: he was, after all, her uncle.

Garrett stared at his tumbler of whiskey before lifting his head to rake his eyes across the room. Callum Ryder-White, looking older than Garrett remembered, stood next to the bar, his once-dark hair now streaked with white. He'd be—what?—in his early eighties now... Garrett paused and did some mental math.

He was thirty-five, so Callum was around forty-eight or -nine when he impregnated his assistant, Garrett's mother, Emma. Callum had been married at the time and had an adult son, James.

Garrett moved his gaze to James. He and his half brother looked like two peas in a pod. Garrett was taller by five inches or so, and more muscular, but there could be no doubt they were related.

It was weird that no one, bar him, had ever picked up on the family resemblance. Well, he presumed his mother saw their similarities, but since she refused to confirm or deny whether Callum was his

father—sparking their two-decades-long cold war—
he couldn't ask her. He tried not to talk to his cold,
ambitious mother any more than he had to.

As the unacknowledged child of ruthless, ambitious and determined Callum Ryder-White and
Emma Kaye, emotionally remote and obsessed with
her position as personal assistant to one of the East
Coast's most powerful men, Garrett was a problem
to be solved, an afterthought and a burden.

He'd learned early on that he was stronger on his
own and that seeking love and approval made one
weak.

But he was thankful for the trust fund that Callum
bequeathed to him on the day he turned twenty-one.
Oh, he couldn't swear on a Bible that it was from
him, but who else would've left Garrett five million dollars? He'd taken that money and invested it
all in an internet start-up business. By the time he'd
finished grad school two years later, his investment
was worth twenty-five million, and the proceeds of
that sale gave him the funds to open Kaye Capital.

His skin prickled remembering the risk he'd
taken. He could've lost everything in one roll of the
dice… He'd gotten lucky. So lucky. He was grateful
his intuition paid off, but a big part of him wanted
to go back and smack his younger self for taking
such a stupid risk. Jesus, he'd had rocks for brains
back then.

But, as his mother said, God protected the young
and dumb.

A burst of laughter pulled him back to the conversation at his table, and he saw Sutton Marchant, best-selling author, and Cody Gallant, owner of a famous events company, wiping tears of laughter from their eyes. Apparently, Jules was a talented storyteller and could charm and entertain.

Garrett was better known for being gruff rather than garrulous.

"I'm looking forward to being involved in the cocktail competition as a judge, Tins. It's such a great idea," Jules stated, looking at Tinsley sitting across the table from her.

"What cocktail competition?" Sutton asked.

Tinsley explained that, as part of their centennial celebrations, Ryder International was sponsoring a contest to find the best cocktail in the world. The competition was open to mixologists and bartenders, the contestants had to make cocktails inspired by world events, and Jules was to be one of their judges.

"What would you make, Ju?" Tinsley asked Jules.

Jules placed her pointed chin on her hand, looking like a bright and bold butterfly. "Mmm, good question. So many things have happened since George Ryder-White opened Ryder's first bar a hundred years ago, and the last century was one of incredible progress and change. The space race, computers, contraception, the internet." She paused, her pretty nose crinkling. "I think I'd do something with equal parts, something feminine and fantastic and fierce, inspired by amazing women who fought for equal rights, women like Ruth Bader Ginsburg, Sojourner Truth, Frida Kahlo and Audre Lorde, among others."

Sutton frowned. "I know who Ginsburg and Kahlo were, but I'm not familiar with Truth and Lorna—"

"*Lorde,*" Garrett corrected him. "Sojourner Truth was born into slavery but escaped and became an outspoken abolitionist who dedicated herself to gender equality. Technically, she's a nineteenth century heroine."

Jules's glare was hot enough to incinerate.

"Audre Lorde was a poet and feminist who, despite being legally blind and having a speech impediment, became an incredible force for change in the movement," he continued.

Jules's eyebrows shot up, and Garrett thought he saw a flash of respect in her eyes. "I'm impressed, Kaye."

Her tone implied the feeling wouldn't last. Garrett felt his lips lift in amusement. "I read."

He read a *lot*, all the time. Reading, he realized at a young age, was an escape from reality, from loneliness, from always feeling on the outside of his mother's life and career. In books, he found new worlds, ideas, concepts and galaxies he could explore to his heart's content.

"The cocktail competition was my dad's idea," Tinsley said. "He's good at coming up with high-concept ideas. He's wasting his talent working for Callum."

No one at the table needed an explanation, as it was common knowledge that Callum Ryder-White kept James on a short leash. Callum was in complete

control of anything and everything that happened at
Ryder International.

Fascinated by Jules's hazel eyes, he watched them
soften to a gentle, warm green-tinged gold as she sent
Tinsley a sympathetic look. Jules was quite fasci-
nating, he thought, sipping his whiskey. Sultry and
sensational. In fact, those adjectives were the perfect
description for Jules Carlson: sultry and sensational.
And, seemingly, sensitive.

He wanted to see her with her clothes off, wrapped
in his sheets. He could see them together—just for
one night, maybe two—but he'd taste her mouth, the
honey between her legs, discover her curves, run his
hands over her skin.

He'd seen her interest when she'd looked at him: it
was in the way she lifted her fingertips to her throat,
the hint of her tongue touching her top lip. She might
not like it—she definitely didn't like him—but she
liked what she saw. Liked the way he made her feel...

Yeah, they'd end up together, maybe tonight,
maybe in two months or two years. He shrugged,
unconcerned at the time line. When you were certain of something, you could wait without worrying.

Jules took a sip from her champagne glass, her
perfectly shaped eyebrows pulling into a thin line.
"I saw that Crazy Kate's Gin is listed as one of the
companies you're considering as sponsors for the
competition. Is that right, Tins?"

Tinsley nodded. "Yeah, as you know, they have
been one of our most important suppliers for the
past few years." She smiled at Jules, her expression

revealing her fondness for her friend. "And Kate introduced us to you, and for that, we'll always be grateful."

Jules's responding smile could power the sun. Garrett felt his sudden intake of breath, the pounding of his blood rushing south. Dammit, that smile should come with a warning, it was that powerful. He wondered what it would feel like under his lips...

"You should rethink Kate as a sponsor, Tinsley, because I doubt they are going to come on board. They have laid off employees and scaled down their operations," Jules explained. Her tone sounded breezy, but the anxiety in her eyes suggested she was downplaying the situation, and he wondered why she would do that.

"What?" Tinsley demanded, shocked. "But why?"

Jules looked a little sick. "So many factors, including the effect of the COVID-19 pandemic."

Garrett noticed that both Cody and Sutton were listening to their conversation. "Crazy Kate's is the one based in North Carolina, right?" Cody asked.

No, it was out west somewhere.

Garrett ran through his mental database of companies, easily pulling up the necessary information. He had a photographic memory, and once he read something, it stayed there forever. Crazy Kate's was a Denver-based boutique gin manufacturer with a small plant and modern, engaging branding. Just before the pandemic, they'd signed loans to expand into what he called the *Big Boy* market, and then lockdown hit. With bars, clubs and restaurants closing, the hospitality sector had taken a hell of a hit. Because he held interests in all sectors of the economy—he believed in having many eggs in many baskets—he'd come through relatively unscathed. That couldn't be said of many businesses.

Jules shook her head. "Denver. Crazy Kate's was the first company I did promotions for. Kate herself suggested that I do pop-up bars. She was instrumental in getting my business off the ground." She looked at Cody. "Ryder's and Crazy Kate's did a joint promotion, and that's how I met Tinsley and Kinga."

Garrett spoke, his deep voice cutting through the buzz of the room. "They recently upgraded their bottling plant, right? And built a brand-new distribution depot?"

He saw their surprise at his knowledge of the small company. As a venture capitalist, companies big, small and in-between were his stock in trade. But he didn't elucidate. He rarely—okay, never— explained anything to anybody.

Jules pointed her spoon in Garrett's direction, her glare hotter than a supernova. "Do not go anywhere near them, Kaye," she told him, her expression fierce.

Right, so he wasn't the only one who read extensively. Judging by her fierce frown, she knew his reputation. As well as being one of the most successful venture capitalists in the world, he was often thought of as someone who preyed on businesses in financial distress by purchasing their debt or their assets at rock-bottom prices and moving them on at a huge profit. It seldom worked that way.

Garrett didn't pull his eyes off Jules, knowing that if he backed down, she'd take that as confirmation of her suspicions.

Sure, he'd made some business decisions that some might call, from the outside looking in, morally ambiguous. He knew he had a reputation for being a flesh-stripping bastard, but sometimes, more often than people realized, some businesses were in such financial distress that the only solution was for someone like him to swoop in and denude the company to cover its debt. Hell, he was often a better bet for the owners than bankruptcy, but his critics were always happy to portray him in a negative light.

Good thing he didn't give a shit.

Garrett saw that Jules was still frowning at him, waiting for a reply to her order to stay away from Crazy Kate's. He lifted his hands in mock surrender. "What? I just asked an innocent question!"

"I only just met you tonight, Kaye, but I suspect that, even as a baby, you weren't innocent," Jules told him, her voice frosty.

In a way, she was right. Emma had never made allowances for his age. He'd never been conned about Santa Claus or the Easter Bunny, told that pixies lived in forests or that the tooth mouse brought you money. No, Emma didn't believe in what she called *all that crap*. Neither had she shielded him from the realities of life. From a young age, he'd been encouraged to watch documentaries and the news and was still haunted by some of the pictures he'd seen.

He wondered whether Jules would be the type of

mom who'd tell her kids about Santa Claus, who'd get up on the roof to make the sound of bells jingling, who'd hide chocolate eggs in the garden for her children to find. Would she slip money under their pillow and put their teeth into a special container and stow it away in a keepsake box? He'd heard that some mothers did that.

Jules was passion and heat and life so…yeah, she'd spin tales of fairies and bunnies, magical mice and a bearded man who brought presents.

"I'm flying out to see Kate next weekend, so I'll see what's going on," Jules told the table, her eyes worried. She bit her bottom lip. "God, I hope she isn't too deep in the hole that she can't find her way out."

Sutton, who in a previous life was a successful trader on Wall Street, sent her a sympathetic smile. "It's probably not as bad as you think," he told her. Garrett, unfortunately, knew better. He had more chance of getting pregnant than Crazy Kate's had of becoming financially viable again.

Jules didn't look convinced. "She's had calls from various companies, offering to buy her debt from the bank."

Sutton exchanged a long look with Garrett, and he saw the question in Sutton's eyes, knew what he was asking. He shook his head. No, he wasn't one of the vultures circling.

"If she agrees to that, she'll lose everything. Her ranch, her savings, everything is tied up in the business," Jules stated, her voice a little wobbly. It was obvious this Kate person meant a great deal to Jules, and Garrett wondered why. It sounded like their relationship went deeper than business. Emotions and business, as he knew, were not happy bedfellows.

"Someone called Volker won't stop calling her," Jules said, not noticing when Tinsley abruptly pushed her chair back and stood up and hurried away. Cody followed her, but Jules, so wrapped up in her subject, was oblivious.

"Do you mean Valder?" Sutton asked, his tone careful.

Hearing the name of his archenemy and industry competitor, Garrett leaned forward and rested his arms on the table. He looked at Sutton, saw the annoyance in his eyes and sighed. Yeah, he didn't always get the best press, but Valder was the king of the vultures, happy to strip businesses of every asset that could turn a profit. Garrett was okay with dismantling businesses and making a buck, but Valder didn't stop there: he also took the shirts off the owners' backs while he was at it. Garrett never advertised his actions and couldn't have people thinking he was a sap, but he always made certain to leave the debt-ridden owners something to show for their hard work, an asset they could build or live on until they got their feet back under them.

Valder was bad news.

"Tell your friend to stay far away from him," Sutton told Jules before standing up. "I'm going to the bar. Can I get either of you another drink?"

They both declined, and then they were alone, sitting opposite each other. Jules lifted her eyes off the bubbles in her champagne to look at him. "Do you agree with him?"

"About Valder? Yeah."

"Is there anything anyone can do?" Jules asked, sounding a little desperate.

He wanted to reassure her but knew that it was better to hurt her with the truth than comfort her with a lie. And what the hell did he know of comfort, anyway? "If Valder is circling, then the situation is dire. He rarely steps in before it's too late."

Jules released a low curse, and Garrett wondered if he'd imagined the gleam in her eyes that suggested tears. "You have a personal relationship with this woman, this Crazy Kate."

The edges of her sexy mouth pulled up at the corners. "Yeah, I do." She pushed back a corkscrew curl, one of two that had been left to hang loose to frame her face. "I spent every summer on her Colorado cattle ranch from the time I was ten. She's my second mom."

Garrett tried to imagine this glamorous woman on a ranch, mucking out stables and wrangling cows. Wrangling cows *was* what they did, wasn't it? Having been brought up in an apartment, he was a city boy to the core and didn't have the first clue. He couldn't imagine this gorgeous woman in her stunning dress shoveling shit. He grinned.

"What's so funny?" Jules demanded, green fire in her eyes again.

"I'm just trying to imagine you on a farm, doing farmy things."

"Farmy things?"

He spread his hands. "Can you ride a horse? Do you know how to muck out a stall?"

Jules rolled her eyes. "And how to service a tractor, break in a horse and plow a field." Her smile turned sinister. "I also know how to castrate a bull."

His balls pulled up and hit the back of his spine. "I'll take your word for that," he replied, annoyed to find his voice an octave higher than it was before. "Seriously? You really know how to do that?"

"And more. You should know that I never lie, Kaye. Ever."

Garrett stared at her, surprised to find his lungs tight and his ability to breathe compromised. He hadn't been this affected by a woman since he'd lost his virginity when he was sixteen. She'd been twenty and, in his eyes, experienced. She'd also lost her shit when she found out—thankfully only after the deed was done—that he was four years younger.

It wasn't his fault he looked older than he was.

But like that long-ago woman, Jules made his heart bounce off his rib cage and his mouth go desert-dry. He felt like he was dancing on the razor-sharp edge of a knife, on the whirling bands of a hurricane. She was dangerous, he realized.

But, damn, what was life without taking the occasional risk?

It wasn't like he was going to hand over his heart to the woman. It was said that he didn't have a heart, and his critics could be right.

The tempo of the music changed, and Garrett

heard the familiar notes of an old standard. It was one of his favorite songs. Few people knew he adored music and that he'd briefly considered studying it as a subject at college. But the thought of being a starving artist didn't appeal so he used music, spending hours at the piano, as a way to de-stress. He tipped his head to the side, waiting for Griff O'Hare to murder the song. But Griff hit the opening note perfectly, and Garrett nodded in appreciation as he sang the lyrics, effortlessly and with emotion. Since the singer was also playing piano, Garrett decided the guy wasn't just a pretty face but a serious musician. His respect for the man inched upward.

Standing up, Garrett rebuttoned his jacket and walked around the table, stopping next to Jules's chair. She looked from his hand to his face, puzzled.

"Are you asking me to dance?"

"Yes. I presume that a woman who can neuter a bull can also sway?"

Her hand slid into his, so much smaller and so much softer. She released a light snort. "Oh, I can do more than sway, Garrett Kaye. I've taken dance classes all my life."

That didn't surprise him. Every movement she made, whether it was to cock her head or lift her hands, was filled with grace. "Is there anything you can't do, Ms. Carlson?"

"Not much," Jules admitted as she stood up. "There are, however, many things I won't do."

He placed his hand on her lower back, keeping his touch light. Her perfume hit his nose, and Garrett was transported to hot summer nights filled with stars and the scent of jasmine.

"What won't you do, Jules?" Garrett asked her, as they hit the edge of the dance floor. He lifted her right hand in his and curled his left around her hip.

"I won't cave-dive, eat guavas or sing in public."

He smiled. "What else?" he asked, a little charmed. And more than a little scared to realize that he could actually *be* charmed.

"Eat snails, bungee jump or pierce my tongue. Oh, and I'm definitely never going to sleep with you."

Garrett Kaye was the most infuriating, irritating, arrogant man she'd ever met.

Yet here she was, in his muscular arms—she could feel the bulge of a big bicep beneath her hand—and inhaling his too-sexy scent, a combination of expensive soap, an even more pricy cologne and testosterone.

Testosterone. Garrett Kaye had it in spades.

Jules lifted her eyes from his perfectly knotted tie and looked at his short beard. His facial hair was at that perfect length between stubble and beard, soft enough to rub your cheek against, short enough for it to tickle in the most delicious way. Jules pulled in a deep breath, held it and released it.

She should not be having salacious thoughts— hell, any thoughts!—about Garrett. He was the embodiment of the type of man she avoided.

She liked slim and small men, gentle men, unambitious men, intelligent men. Okay, Garrett was

obviously smart—one didn't reach his level of success without some smarts—and he was well-read,
but he was too blunt, too direct, too damn masculine.

Too damn alpha…

Too much like her dad.

Big, bold and overconfident men didn't interest
her, and he embodied all three.

But, damn, her body wasn't getting her brain's
warning signals. Her left hand wanted to trace the
curve of his huge shoulder, and she kept reminding
herself that she couldn't move closer, that she must
not press her aching-to-be-touched breasts against
his acre-wide chest. Her stomach kept doing a slow
roll, and the space between her legs felt like it was
on fire. Her body wanted him, but her brain was urg-
ing her to run for cover.

Garrett's thumb brushed the bare skin on her
lower back, and Jules shivered. "I can't decide
whether that's a good shiver or a bad one," Garrett
said, his deep voice sliding inside her and turning
her blood to hot molasses.

Jules tipped her head back to look into his aston-
ishing eyes, blue with more than a touch of teal. "I'm
not sure what you mean," she said, happy to hear that
her voice sounded like it normally did.

Another swipe of that thumb, another shiver. "I
think you are attracted to me, but your brain is flashing ten-foot warning signals, telling you to run."

Jules stopped abruptly, shocked at his perception.
She pulled her hand from his and took a step back.
"Why would you think that?" she demanded. Did

the guy have X-ray vision? Was looking below the surface his superpower?

She didn't like it. At all.

Garrett picked up her hand again and pulled her back into his embrace.

She was ironing-board stiff but she couldn't unbend, because if she did, she might be tempted to snuggle in and rest against that broad chest, to feel safe.

Nobody else could protect her; she was responsible for her safety. That was why she held a black belt in judo and knew how to use a knife. She stayed away from guns, as having one put to your temple as a six-year-old tended to lead to a lifelong hatred of them.

"Come back to me right now, Jules," Garrett ordered her. "Wherever you are is not the place you want to be."

Jules's eyes flew up to meet his, and her mouth dropped open in shock. How could he possibly know that she was back in their kitchen in Detroit, that her mom was begging her dad to let her go, telling her that she'd do anything—*anything!*—if she didn't hurt their little girl.

Her dad had flung Jules away and grabbed her mom's arm, and the two-hundred-fifty-pound man had dragged her tiny mom to their bedroom. The next day, as soon as her dad had left for work, she and her mom left town and hit the road.

In the following months and years, Jules got very used to moving, very quickly. It was now a habit, and instead of bouncing from town to town, she bounced between countries and continents.

Garrett gave her hand a quick squeeze. "Are you okay, Ju— What's your real name, by the way?"

She blinked at the sudden change of subject. "Juliana-Jaliyah, hyphenated." Whoa.

Only a handful of people knew her real name: she was Jules to her friends and Joolz, no surname, when she was working and on all her social-media accounts.

Why on earth had she told Garrett Kaye her real name?

"Juliana-Jaliyah… That's quite a mouthful."

"Tell me about it," she muttered. "And I had a lisp."

Garrett's sexy mouth pulled up into what had to be the first real smile she'd seen from him this evening. It hit his eyes, made the crinkles at the corners deepen and turned the teal blue lighter and greener. Yeah, he should laugh more. He was a masculine type of beautiful when he laughed.

"It's a mouthful but a pretty mouthful. And it suits you."

Jules poked him in the chest. "Everybody calls me Jules," she told him. Nobody ever called her by her full name. Since her teens, she'd introduced herself as Jules. It was stronger, a name that kicked ass.

"When I was young, I went through a stage of refusing to answer to any name other than Hedwig."

It took her a while to make the connection. "The famous owl from *Harry Potter*?"

His big shoulders rose and fell. "I liked to read. And waging war with my mother. I'd bring back books from the library, and she'd look at them and decide they weren't age-appropriate."

She smiled, intrigued. "Like?"

"Well, I do remember her having a shit fit when I brought home *Go Ask Alice* at twelve."

Jules winced, remembering the book's themes of drug use, rape and sexual abuse. She could just imagine the tug-of-war. "Who won the argument?"

Garrett flashed a grin that would have looked more at home on a pirate. "Neither, or both. I read the controversial books at the library and brought home the books that I wanted to read and knew she'd approve of."

"Smart, willful and a little arrogant," Jules commented. She lifted her eyebrows. "Nothing much has changed in—what?—twenty-eight years?"

"I'm thirty-five, not forty…" Garrett muttered.

Jules hid her smile at his annoyance. "Really? You look older," she lied.

"Haha, funny. What were you like at twelve?"

Introverted, scared, scarred. Jules tossed her head and looked him dead in the eye. "Fabulous and flirty. And absolutely nothing has changed," she stated, her voice defiant. Nobody but Kate knew about her childhood, not even Tinsley and Kinga, her best friends.

Garrett's eyes bored into hers. "Liar," he softly responded. He moved their joined hands so that the knuckle of his thumb rested on her bottom lip. Jules resisted the urge to touch the tip of her tongue to his skin.

"Why do I think that your supposedly fabulous life—I did a quick online search under the table while Callum Ryder-White did his speech—is carefully constructed? You *want* the world to think you are this carefree creature with the world at her feet."

Jules stared at him, her heart in her throat. "Why would you think that?"

He shrugged and dropped their hands. "Your bio is littered with words like *nomadic*, *interesting*, and *free and easy* and gives the impression that you are happy-go-lucky and insouciant. You're not."

Wow. He'd just stabbed through her layers, his words piercing her carefully crafted cloak. She was both fascinated and horrified but couldn't resist her next question.

"So who do you think I am, then, O Wise One?" Jules intended her tone to be mocking but wasn't sure she hit her target. She sounded a little off balance and, worst of all, a tiny bit scared.

"I think the world sees your beautiful face and rocking body and gets sucked in by your bright, bubbly personality and decides that's who you are."

"So who do *you* think I am, Kaye?" Jules challenged him. And why did she care?

"Honestly, every time I look into your constantly changing eyes, I get this impression of a woman who's walked through hell and has come out the other side, pulling a tank of water in case of random flames."

The music stopped, and so did Jules's ability to breathe. No one had ever, in so short a time, found all her protective layers and pushed them aside to get to the heart of her. Who was this man with his wizard-like abilities?

Before she could gather her words, Garrett dropped his hand from her back and stepped away. He pulled their still-linked hands to his mouth and kissed the ridge of her knuckles. "Thank you for the dance. And, Juliana-Jaliyah?"

"Yes?"

"We *are* going to sleep together. Sooner rather than later, and you will be the one doing the asking."

Then he walked away, leaving her speechless and discombobulated on the edge of the dance floor.

Two

Garrett didn't want to leave Jules—why would he when she was both gorgeous and interesting, the best combination?—but he'd noticed James Ryder-White's eyes following him around the dance floor.

What was up with that? Why was he the focus of his half brother's attention?

Because he was a guy who preferred to confront a situation rather than walk away and worry about it, he thought it was time that he and James had a little talk. Oh, he wouldn't tell James what he suspected— that they were related—as he'd made a promise to his mother a long time ago that he would never raise the subject of his parentage with any Ryder-White, ever.

He regretted making that promise, but he still intended to keep it.

That long-ago argument with his mom was the root of their still-dysfunctional relationship. They weren't estranged. They still occasionally spoke, but since that summer, they didn't venture beyond inquiries about each other's health and the weather. And whenever they found themselves alone, it wasn't long before a two-ton elephant strolled into the room and plopped itself in the corner...

I know who my father is, Mom. Why won't you confirm it?

I don't have to confirm a damn thing and never will.

Unlike many people, he hadn't found a letter or his birth certificate or read any of his mom's private correspondence. No, his discovery of his father's identity was completely random, the strangest, weirdest fluke.

A few weeks after he'd turned sixteen, he'd swung by her office to pick up her bank card—visiting her at work was strongly discouraged!—because his had expired, and he couldn't use it to do the grocery run, one of his many chores.

She'd been angry at his sudden appearance and had told him to wait in the break room, telling him she'd get to him as soon as she could. Wanting to be outside, he'd walked onto the balcony off the break room and, as he always did when he walked from a dark room into sunlight, released a huge sneeze.

He waited forty-five minutes, becoming increasingly more irritated. His vigil was broken when his mom's boss, Callum Ryder-White, walked outside, too, and, like him, immediately sneezed into a snow-white handkerchief.

Because he'd been a brat and thought that every-body wanted to hear his opinions, he'd informed Callum that sneezing in sunlight was called ACHOO, or Autosomal Dominant Compelling Helio-Opthalmic Outburst. He'd been about to tell Callum that he had it, too, but the man's ice-blue eyes and why-are-you-talking-to-me look cut off Garrett's words. His mom hurried onto the balcony at that point, apologized to Callum for her son's presence—children of staff members were not welcome at Ryder Tower—and shoved some money into his hand and told him to beat it.

But Callum walked ahead of him, and Garrett couldn't help noticing that as he walked, Callum repeatedly touched his right index finger to his thumb...

It was a nervous tic that Garrett had, too.

On returning home, he went online and, because Callum was one of the best-known businesspeople on the East Coast, saw photographs of him when he was a young man. Like Garrett, Callum was tall, and their face structures were the same. They had the same bold nose and deep-set eyes. Garrett could dismiss their physical similarities, but a little further research told him that the ACHOO syndrome was mostly inherited...

His mom didn't have it, so it had to come from his father.

Garrett and Emma had their first fight about his

parentage that evening, and their fights over her lack of honesty and transparency didn't stop until he left for college. She did, however, manage to elicit that promise from him not to say anything about his suspicions to anybody, ever.

Garrett took his promises seriously so, to this day, his hands were tied.

Garrett slid into the empty spot next to James, rested his elbows on the bar and ordered a fifteen-year-old whiskey.

"Care to tell me why you are watching me?" Garrett demanded.

James jerked at his blunt question, obviously caught off guard. He scrambled for an answer. "I've known Jules for a long time. She's Tinsley's best friend, and I'm protective of her."

Good catch. "And you think she needs protection from me?"

James nodded. "Something like that."

"Bullshit," Garrett retorted. "First of all, Jules needs no help. Her tongue is more effective than industrial-strength paint stripper. And you weren't looking at her, you were looking at me."

It seemed to Garrett that James was using a hell of a lot of willpower to keep his expression impassive. "If you say so," he said, allowing a trace of derision to touch his voice.

Was that snotty voice supposed to intimidate him? Sure, his half brother was nearly twenty-five years older than him, but if Garrett allowed himself to be intimidated by men who had years on him, he wouldn't own and manage a multibillion dollar company.

Garrett sipped from the glass the bartender slid his way and looked over it at James. "Why have I caught your attention, James? Why am I in your crosshairs?"

Shock jumped into James's eyes. Gotcha, Garrett thought. What was going through his half sibling's head, and how did it affect him? He looked down, saw the tremor in James's fingers and frowned. Something was bubbling under his seemingly calm surface. He reminded Garrett of one of those prank cans, the ones that, when opened, shot out a snake or a clown.

Garrett saw that the two men on the other side of James were far too interested in their conversation, so he lowered his voice. "Why do I sense that you, the son of my mother's boss—" Yep, something flared in his eyes with that comment. James definitely knew more than he let on. Join the freakin' club. "—can disrupt my life?"

He was fishing here, hoping that James would let slip something to confirm his suspicions that they were related. And if he did, what would Garrett do with that information? He wasn't angling to become part of a family—he had no idea how to be a son, a brother or an uncle. Hell, his mother had barely allowed him to be a son. They'd been two strangers living in the same house for much of his life. His mom was physically present, but she'd been consumed with her job, with her position as Callum's right-hand person.

He'd been very young, too young, when he first realized that Callum and her career were higher up on her priority list than he was.

No, a family wasn't for him. But he wouldn't mind knowing if there were any health concerns he needed to be aware of. He already had ACHOO. Was there anything else he'd inherited from his father? Didn't he have a right to know that information?

Garrett sighed, turned and looked across the room to see Jules dancing with Sutton Marchant. He was laughing, she was laughing, and they looked good together. Garrett felt the intense urge to plow his fist into Sutton's aristocratic face.

Mine! Mine! Mine!

Crap, if they could hear his thoughts, every feminist in the country would strip him of a few layers of skin. Women were not possessions; men didn't get to own them. He knew this—of course he did; he wasn't a Neanderthal. He didn't have gender, racial or any other kind of pay gaps at his firm: as far as he was concerned, if you did the same job, you earned the same salary. Promotions were based on performance. Anyone, male or female, who engaged in sexual harassment got their asses fired.

So why did he want to storm across the room and haul Jules out of Sutton's arms and drag her into his? Garrett ran his hand over his jaw. He was losing his goddamn mind. No, he'd lost his mind when he agreed to pay a stupid amount of cash to attend this super exclusive event. Mind gone, he was now descending into madness. It was the only rational explanation.

Even from a distance, he could see that Jules was back to being her charming, charismatic self. But it wasn't her, not really. Charming Jules was a carefully concocted version of herself, the person she thought the world wanted to see.

Juliana-Jaliyah was deeper, smarter, and she was, like him, scratched and scarred.

"I'm not aiming anything at you, Garrett," James said.

Garrett turned back to look at James, taking a minute to make sense of his words. He felt shocked that just looking at Jules could shift his laserlike focus.

"My gut is insisting that you are up to something, and it's never failed me before," Garrett told him, getting his thoughts back in the game.

"Maybe your Spidey sense is wrong," James suggested. James didn't sound as confident as he had a few minutes before. Garrett thought that he might've inadvertently stumbled across something here.

Yeah, this ball was turning out to be far more interesting than he'd expected.

"It's never wrong," Garrett retorted, banging his glass on the bar. He looked down at James— thanks to his height, he pretty much looked down on everyone—knowing his eyes had turned dark and dangerous. They always did when he was upset. Or frustrated.

"What's going on, James? What are you thinking, planning? Want to save me the hassle and tell me now?"

James opened his mouth to speak but slammed his jaw closed again, so hard that Garrett thought it might hurt.

"I think you have either had too much to drink or have an overactive imagination, Garrett."

Garrett shook his head. "Nah, that's not it." Garrett clamped his hand around James's shoulder and squeezed. "You don't have to tell me. I'm good at ferreting out secrets, and I'll discover yours."

James looked like he'd popped the lid on that gag can, but the snake inside it was real. And poisonous.

Interesting, Garrett thought, walking away.

Jules smiled at Sutton as he pulled her hand through his crooked elbow and led her off the dance floor. He was a nice guy, and dancing with him had been fun…

But he was not, in any way, compelling. She wasn't attracted to Sutton, not like she was to Garrett Kaye. Being up close and personal with Garrett's spectacular body made her feel like she was plugged into an electrical socket. Her body—stupid thing!—craved his.

But conversing with him made her feel like she was jamming an acid-tipped fork into her eye.

She'd beg him to sleep with her? When unicorns made a comeback and she could hire Snow White's dwarves to clean her apartment.

And, let's be clear here, she didn't like his ability to see past her skillfully molded public persona to whom she was below. Not that he'd managed to peel off too many layers, but he'd definitely gotten further than most.

Irritating man.

Jules saw Kinga standing next to the stage, holding a champagne glass against her chest, swaying as she watched her fiancé sing. Jules grabbed her elbow and tugged her away.

"Hey, that's one of my favorite songs!" Kinga protested when they stopped in a quiet corner of the ballroom, far away from the bar and the dance floor.

"I love you, King, but since meeting Griff, you've turned into such a sap," Jules told her, rolling her eyes.

Kinga's grin told her that she wasn't offended. "I know! But he's so talented and so hot, and he does this thing that just—"

Jules placed a hand over her mouth and shook her head so hard that her curls bounced. "No, no, no, *no*! I do not need to know what kinky stuff you get up to, thank you very much!"

Kinga peeled her hand off her mouth, grinning. "You are such a prude!"

No, she wasn't. Or at least she didn't think she was. Okay, she didn't *want* to be a prude…

What would Garrett think if she told him that she was one of the few twenty-eight-year-old virgins left in the Western world? Would he laugh, mock her, denigrate her? Or would he see her as a challenge? Really, his notion that she'd beg him to take her to bed was laughable.

It would never happen.

But she was annoyingly tempted. She wanted to peel back his layers of clothing and see if that big body was as fit as he felt, if she was exaggerating the circumference of his big biceps and if she could curl up on his chest.

She was a smart, independent, capable woman—life had taught her to be that way—so why did she look at him and think...*protector*? She didn't need one of those, just like she didn't need a husband or a significant other. She was fine on her own. Better than fine: she was *safe*.

After being chased around the country by her obsessive and possessive father, knowing that if he caught them, they might end up, well...*dead*, feeling safe was high on her list of priorities. And, yeah, she now had issues. And one of those was sex...

No, that was wrong. She didn't have a problem with sex per se—at least she didn't think she did, as she'd gotten pretty damn intimate with a few guys—but she did have a problem with bedrooms. And that was where most guys thought sex should take place.

Jules didn't like bedrooms. It was where bad things happened behind closed doors.

Grunts, screams, tears, sobs. Fists hitting flesh...

As far as Jules was concerned, bedrooms were only good for storing clothes. She hadn't slept in a bed behind a closed door since they'd left Detroit more than twenty years ago.

And she liked it that way.

Jules looked across the ballroom and, because he

was so tall, immediately spotted Garrett. Her stomach rocketed up to her throat and plummeted down to her toes, and her skin prickled with goose bumps. And annoyingly, she felt that insistent tingle between her legs. Normally, when her body reminded her that she was a woman in her sexual prime, she used a vibrator to take the edge off. Jules winced, remembering that it was in a box in her cupboard gathering dust. She'd been busy lately, running from country to country and city to city, and she was usually too tired to feel horny.

But tonight, she was beyond horny. She wanted to *jump him now.*

She might think he was gorgeous, but she didn't like him and especially didn't like how perceptive he was. But for the first time, her body's desire was strong enough to dampen her mind's insistence on caution, its need to keep her safe.

But Jules knew, deep down inside where truth resided, that Garrett Kaye—he of the sharp mind and blunt tongue—would never, ever hurt her.

Kinga lightly pinched her wrist, and Jules jumped. "What?"

"You dragged me over here, remember? And now you're just standing there, staring off into space," Kinga replied. Jules turned to look at her, and her eyes immediately softened, and she ran her hand up and down Jules's bare arm. "Are you okay, honey? What's up?"

Jules played with her thick, faux-diamond-and-beaded bangle. "Weird evening, that's all."

"Are you not liking the people at your table?" Kinga asked, immediately concerned. "I thought that sitting with Cody and Tinsley would be where you'd be happiest."

While she earned a good living, she wasn't in the can-spend-the-price-of-a-house-to-buy-a-ticket bracket. Ryder International, or, to be precise, her friends, comped her ticket to the ball. They'd told her that they'd be happy to give her another complimentary ticket so she could bring a date, but Jules hadn't wanted to take advantage of their friendship. Besides, she wasn't dating anyone—she didn't have time for that ritual—and wouldn't invite some random man to such an exclusive event.

"It's not that, Kinga." Well, it was partly that. Jules sucked in some air and tipped her head back to look at the fabric-swathed ceiling. "Do you know Garrett Kaye?"

Kinga frowned. "Sort of. I mean, I've met the guy a few times. Gorgeous but not chatty."

A perfect summation. "We've been trading barbs all evening, and I danced with him. There's some sort of weird chemistry bubbling between us."

Kinga's eyebrows flew up. "Really? I didn't think you were his type."

Not his type? What the hell did that mean? "Because I'm of mixed heritage?" Jules demanded.

Kinga waved her words away. "No, you know I don't mean that! What I meant was that, according to the East Coast gossips, Garrett always chooses a very particular type of woman when he's looking for a date to an event or to grace his bed."

"And what type is that?" Jules asked.

"Cool, snotty, someone with impeccable connections and an amazing pedigree."

Kinga made them sound like the nonhuman entrants in a Crufts dog show.

"You couldn't be more different. And different, might I remind you, is good," Kinga added.

"How can I want to jump his bones when I don't know him? And the little I know, I don't like!"

"People have sex for different reasons, Jules. Sometimes that reason is love, a soul-deep connection with a partner. Sometimes that reason is stress relief, a need to feel connected to another human being. And sometimes because it just feels so damn good!"

Jules placed her hands behind her back and rested her palms against the wall. "I don't have casual sex, Kinga. I'm not cut out for it."

"You've never had a one-night stand?"

"Uh…no." She felt the urge to tell Kinga that she'd never had penetrative sex, but she held back. Would her friend even believe her? She liked men, she dated all the time, she'd received and given oral sex, but whenever a potential lover suggested they take it to the bedroom, she called a halt to proceedings. As a result, men faded from her life as mist did from mountains on a hot summer's day.

Kinga cocked her head to one side, thinking. "You like olives, right?"

"Yes."

"And anchovies?"

"You know I do." Where was Kinga going with this?

"And you hate snails."

Jules shuddered. "Yuck."

"How did you know that you liked those foods? By trying them, right? So give a one-night stand a go. If you don't like it, because not everyone does, don't do it again." Kinga squeezed her hand. "But there's no shame, either way, Ju. Your body, your rules. No exceptions to that rule, *ever.*"

It was excellent advice, Jules thought as she followed Kinga back to the main area of the ballroom. But maybe, before she ventured down the one-night-stand road, she should have sex first: penetrative sex.

That, she thought, should be step number one. But allowing Garrett to be her first would be a mistake. He was someone who'd expect his partner to be experienced, to know what the hell they were doing in bed. He'd have no patience for an inexperienced virgin, and she didn't want to feel like a fumbling idiot.

But she didn't want to sleep with anyone else.

Catch-22, she thought.

Marvelous.

Nearly a month had passed since the Valentine's Day Ball, yet to Garrett, it felt like last week. He'd spent most of the last two weeks crisscrossing the country, and he was glad to be spending Friday morning in his office, catching up.

After a crack-of-dawn five-mile run, he'd made the minute commute to his office from his penthouse apartment on the top floor of his office building, determined to work through his mile-long to-do list. But being back in Portland—wet and cold—made him think about Jules, where she was and what she was up to.

According to her social-media pages, which he, embarrassingly, checked every day, she was currently stateside and taking a minibreak from demonstrations and manning pop-up bars in exotic cities like Cartagena and Cape Town. She was taking the weekend, maybe the week, she told her million-plus followers. She needed to breathe deep, slow down, do a digital detox.

She'd been on his mind, more than he'd expected. She'd pop in at random times—while he was inspecting a plant, or in the middle of a cash-flow projection—and he'd remember her lithe body in his arms, the feel of her golden skin under his hand as they danced, her dizzy-making scent.

Thoughts of her had even prompted him to make inquiries into Crazy Kate's, and he'd winced when he'd received detailed reports from his most experienced researcher. The company was so far in the hole they were knocking on hell's door...

They'd run out of cash, creditors were baying, and the bank had given them minimal time to make a massive balloon payment. Because her house, buildings and the ranch Jules mentioned were mortgaged to the hilt, Kate had more chance of taking a magic-carpet ride than she did of making that payment.

To save the company, she needed an angel investor, someone who was prepared to put a load of cash into the organization and not see results for five, maybe ten, years, if they ever did at all. It was that far gone…and nobody he knew, including him, was fool enough to touch it with a barge pole. Even Valder had backed off, knowing that there wasn't enough value in the assets to cover the debt.

Kate was facing bankruptcy and the loss of everything she owned. It was a scenario he'd seen played out so often before. Sad but inevitable.

Jules, he was sure, would be devastated to learn that the ranch would leave Kate's hands. It was obvious, to him at least, that she had an emotional connection to the property and that she loved Kate. He wondered how they'd met, how an East Coast girl had come to spend time on a ranch in Colorado.

He spent an enormous amount of time—far too much—wondering about Jules Carlson.

Garrett lifted his head at a discreet knock on his door. His assistant stepped into his office, the sleeves of his button-down rolled up past his elbows, displaying colorful ink. Sven refused to wear anything other than jeans. He had two piercings through his right eyebrow, a ring through his lower lip and a stud in his cheek. He was built like a tank, and he had the most extensive vocabulary of curse words of anyone Garrett knew.

He also had a postgraduate degree in ancient languages, could tiptoe into any computer anywhere in the world and was the most efficient, organized soul Garrett had ever encountered. They had an understanding. He organized Garrett's life, occasionally did some not-always-legal digital breaking and entering, and managed his office with startling efficiency.

Garrett's part of the deal was to pay him an enormous salary—he was worth every penny—and not give him any crap about his clothing choices, piercings and tats. Garrett also gave him an afternoon off a week to visit his brother who lived in a residential home for people with intellectual disabilities, and Garrett had to fund Sven's addiction to expensive coffee.

It was a deal that worked for both of them.

"What's up?" Garrett asked as Sven dropped into a chair opposite his desk.

Sven nodded at his stack of requisition forms. "Accounting is bugging me for those."

Garrett pulled a face. "I'm getting there." He'd get there faster if he stopped thinking about Jules.

"You wanted to keep your day free of appointments, but James Ryder-White wants to meet with you. He wouldn't tell me why, but he insisted it was important."

Shock flashed over Garrett, then curiosity. He'd vowed to dig into James: he knew the man was up to something, but the month had run away from him.

"You heard that Callum Ryder-White had a heart attack, right?" Sven asked.

He hadn't. He lifted his eyebrows. "When did that happen?"

"A week, ten days ago? Apparently, it's quite serious. He's going to be out of the office for a while."

"He should've retired years ago," Garrett told him. His father was in the hospital, and Emma hadn't bothered to tell him. Then again, he hadn't spoken to his mom for six weeks—or was it eight? Garrett ran a hand over his face. Man, they were the definition of *dysfunctional*.

"So, do you want to meet with James? And when?"

Garrett leaned back in his chair, propped his feet up on his desk and stared up at the ceiling. It was his favorite thinking position. He was curious as to why James, who had to have his hands full running Ryder International, was asking for an urgent meeting. With him. Of all people.

Why?

And that's why he'd meet with his half brother: because he was so damn curious. But he'd meet when it would be convenient for him, not James. "He can come by, but later. Kaye Capital business comes first."

"Around six?"

Garrett nodded. "That'll work. Anything else?"

Sven nodded to the requisitions. "Yeah, those. Marge needs them, and you know she scares the hell out of me." Garrett rolled his eyes. Nobody scared Sven, not even him.

Sven lumbered to his feet and headed to the door.

"Is there any chance of getting a decent cup of coffee?" Garrett asked him.

"When you are done with those reqs," Sven told him. At Garrett's scowl, he grinned. "Everybody needs motivation, even you."

"How about this for motivation? Make me a cup of coffee, or else I'm going to fire your ass. Or cut off your supply of Jamaican Blue," Garrett mildly suggested.

They both knew that the threat of losing the supply of his favorite coffee was the direr of the two options. "Requisitions first, coffee later," Sven told him, closing the door behind him.

Garrett glared at his closed door, muttered a curse and picked up his pen. He was about to dash his name across the bottom of the page when his smartphone signaled an incoming message. Garrett picked it up and swiped the screen, frowning. Few people had this number, and most messages came through to the cell phone Sven managed for him.

He opened the messaging app and saw an unfamiliar number but when he tapped the profile picture, a very familiar face appeared on his screen. His heart lurched as he took in Jules Carlson's fresh and lovely face. In the photo her eyes looked green, her curls hung down the sides of her face, and he could see tiny freckles on her nose and across those amazing cheekbones.

God, she was stunning.

Garrett, I heard that you are back in town and was wondering if we could meet. I'll buy you a drink.

Whatever time and wherever suits. It's rather urgent. Jules Carlson.

Garrett wanted to think she was asking him out on a date, hopefully to bed, but he knew he was chasing rainbows. There was a formality to her message, an underlying tension he hadn't expected.

She wanted something from him, and he suspected that it had something to do with Kate Kennedy of Crazy Kate's.

But, hell, he didn't care. She'd reached out, and he'd meet her, anytime and anywhere.

What about at the Portland Harbor bar around eight?

That would give him an hour with James, twenty minutes to freshen up and twenty minutes to get to the hotel. He only needed ten. Her reply came a few minutes later, just a thumbs-up. Yep, definitely not a date.

Garrett sighed. Crap, he thought, as he dashed his signature across the bottom of the page of a requisition which he hadn't actually read.

The woman fried his brain cells, and if they got to bed, he had no doubt she'd short-circuit his brain.

He had to be careful with this one.

Three

Across town, in the exquisitely decorated living room in his wing of Callum's estate, James paced the area in front of the fireplace, listening for the sound of Penelope's footsteps.

He wiped his damp palms on his thighs and stared into the fire, not hearing the hiss and crack of the burning wood.

James placed his forearm on the marble mantel and stared down at his five-hundred-dollar shoes. This was not going to be a fun conversation, but it needed to be held, things needed to be said.

They couldn't keep living like this.

He couldn't keep living like this.

James strode over to the art deco drinks trolley, picked up the crystal decanter and sloshed a hefty amount of whiskey into a tumbler. He tossed the liquor back, gasped at the burn and poured himself another glass.

He needed liquid courage…

Penelope stepped into the room, tall and slim and effortlessly graceful. She raised her eyebrows at his whiskey glass and looked at the diamond-encrusted watch—Piaget? Cartier?—on her delicate wrist. It was a silent rebuke, and James flushed.

Yeah, it was midmorning, but there were times when a man needed help to get him through a conversation. This was one of them.

James gestured to the cream-colored sofa. "Take a seat. Can I get you a drink?"

"It's far too early for me," Penelope replied, sending him a cool look. His aristocratic, cool-as-mountain-water wife had a way of castigating him without saying a word, and still, after more than three decades of marriage, could make him feel like an awkward teenager.

It was her superpower.

James hitched up the fabric of his trousers and sat down opposite her, turning his head to look out onto the cove below them. He loved this property on Cousin's Island with its massive house, private stretch of beach and purpose-built marina, and he'd imagined he'd grow old here, looking at his view.

But if he put his plan into action, everything that was familiar, including this house, would be taken away.

But he'd be free.

"You asked to speak to me, James," Pen said. When he looked at her, he saw the hint of a frown between her jet-black eyebrows, her tense full mouth and the anxiety in her eyes. She was still a beautiful woman and looked like Tinsley and Kinga's sister rather than their mother.

Looking good, her position in East Coast society and being married to the heir of the Ryder-White fortune were important to Penelope and had been some of the main reasons she'd married him in the late eighties. James didn't think much had changed since then.

He tapped his index finger against his knee. How should he start this difficult conversation? "I'm considering challenging the status quo."

Penelope's gaze sharpened. "And what, exactly, does that mean?"

He gathered all the courage he had. "I've been thinking about what Tinsley said about secrets a few weeks back, how the truth needs to come out," James stated. "I think she's right. I think there are a bunch of Ryder-White secrets that need to see the light."

Penelope placed her hand on her chest and played with the pearl pendant on her thick gold chain, something she only did when she was feeling nervous. The observation calmed him; it was good to know that he wasn't the only one feeling off balance.

"We are rapidly heading toward retirement, and we've danced to Callum's tune all our lives, Pen. I'm sick of it."

"Our dancing ensured that we had access to this

house, to a certain standard of living," Penelope pointed out. "It allowed us to send our girls to the best colleges, to set up trust funds for them."

"I think that's what Callum's trained us to believe," James responded. He'd been thinking about this, a lot.

"I was twentysomething when I took my uncle Ben's side against Callum, and at the time he told me I'd pay for my disloyalty. For thirty-plus years, Callum's pushed the guilt button, the you're-a-useless-son button, the you're-nothing-without-me button. And I believed him," James responded. God, being honest, with one's spouse and with oneself, was both hurtful and liberating.

"I've been conditioned to believe that we would be nowhere without Callum. He's always said that he and Ryder International are the sources of all our good fortune, but that's not true."

Penelope cocked her head and gestured for him to continue.

"We've bought and sold property all our lives, and we've made some tidy investments, made quite a bit of money independent of Callum." He'd been the one to play the property market but thought it advantageous to include her in the statement. "That's how I set up trusts for the girls, good trusts." And the trust for Garrett.

"What's your point, James?"

James uncrossed his legs and placed his arms on his forearms. "I'm tired of dancing to Callum's tune, Pen. I want to live my own life…"

Penelope held her thick gold rope in a tight grip. "Are you asking for a divorce?"

Her voice never wavered, but he saw the nervousness in her eyes. They weren't the happiest couple in the world, but they rubbed along well enough. He'd had a couple of mistresses and had never asked or wanted to know whether she'd had lovers herself. Some questions were better left unanswered.

"No, I'm not asking for a divorce." He saw her shoulder slump in relief, and his ego grinned. "I just want to step away from Callum, live our own lives on our terms."

"If you do that, you'll lose your inheritance. So will the girls."

"What, exactly, will we lose, Pen?" James demanded.

Her answer came quickly. "The Ryder-White shares, the art and car collections, the access to the apartments in London and France, the investments. This house."

"When did we last use the European apartments?" James replied, trying to keep his tone mild. "I don't even know what's in the art collection. It's tucked away in a climate-controlled warehouse, and even if Callum did grant me access, everything is wrapped up and hidden away. Callum never allows anyone into the facility where he keeps his collection of rare and classic cars. God knows the last time any of them were driven. Besides, how many cars can we drive at one time?"

"And this house?"

"I'll miss this house, of course I will. But we have other houses, and we have money, lots of it. If we need to, we can rent a hotel suite in Paris and London and stay as long as we like, and we can spend hours in museums and galleries looking at fantastic art."

He pushed a hand through his graying hair. "Callum has never allowed me to make any decisions about the company. It's never felt like mine, anyway," James told her. "I'd rather be free than be controlled by him anymore."

"And the girls?" Penelope asked.

It was a fair question, and most of his worries centered around them.

"I've spent so much time thinking about how this will impact them. If I walk, they won't inherit anything from Callum—"

"They are girls. They wouldn't have inherited anyway," Penelope said, her words bitter.

True enough.

"They are both wealthy in their own right and are exceptionally well educated. They'll inherit millions from us when we die. They have also found the men who make them happy. Wealthy men, I might add. If I walk away and Callum fires them in retaliation, they could open up a PR business and make a killing all on their own. None of us *need* Callum." James looked away from her and stared down at his hands. "I am almost sixty years old, and I need to be my own man, Pen. I also need to know you'd support me in that."

Penelope stood up and walked away from him

to stand by the bay window. She placed her hand on the glass and stared down at the gunmetal gray water churning in the bay below. "I'm not opposed to your idea, James. You can walk away, right now, today, and I'd go with you, if that's what you want," she stated.

Yes, that's what he wanted.

"Except you've overlooked one important factor. When Callum dies, everything will come to you, anyway. You'd still have the responsibility of everything. Whether it's today or ten years from now, it's going to be yours, and walking away now won't change that. You are Callum's only male heir."

And there it was, the opening he needed. James stared at Penelope, and she knew him well enough to know that there was something she was missing. "What?" she demanded.

He simply looked at her, waiting for her to connect the dots on her own. Then her eyes widened, and the color in her face faded. "There's another heir out there, one that you know of," she whispered.

One that you know of... Did he imagine her emphasis on the *you*? He pushed the thought aside. It wasn't important, not right now. James sucked in some much-needed air and gathered his courage.

"Garrett Kaye is my son. That's why I'm meeting with him tonight to suggest he take over as CEO of Ryder International. If I acknowledge him as mine, if he acknowledges me as his father, I assume that Callum will immediately change his will, and I will be edged out. I'm okay with that."

Penelope held up her hand. *"Wait! What?* Garrett is your son?"

"We'd need a DNA test to confirm it, but yeah, he's mine." James explained the circumstances of his birth, that he found out he was a father after their marriage. "Emma would not admit he was my child, and I kept demanding answers. She wouldn't discuss Garrett with me, and I wouldn't drop the subject so she threatened to tell you and Callum, and the police, that I'd raped her. I couldn't risk the gossip and the nastiness, so I backed off."

"That bitch!"

Yep, he agreed.

"I love our daughters, you know I do, but I've missed out on thirty-five years with my son. I'd like to get to know him, if he'll let me." James stood up and jammed his shaking hands into the pockets of his suit pants. Pen looked as shocked as he'd expected her to: her face was ghost-white, and a fine tremor racked her slim frame. But she was holding up better than he'd thought, and he was proud of his strong wife.

He wanted to go to her, to pull her into his arms and comfort her, but he knew she needed time to take in this earthshaking news. She wouldn't yell or scream—Pen wasn't dramatic—but she'd need time to process what she'd heard.

"If you tell me that I can't acknowledge him, that you don't want to rock the boat, I'll respect that. We'll just keep on keeping on as we've done for the past three and a half decades." He'd be disappointed, but he'd learned to live with that particular emotion.

"And neither of us will be happy," Penelope whispered.

James shrugged. They hadn't been happy for a long, long time. That was the price they'd paid for him standing up to his father, for taking his uncle's side when Ben told Callum that he'd never marry, that he was in love with, and wanted to marry, another man.

Penelope dug her nails into her biceps and looked at him, her expression reflecting her bone-deep fear.

"I know you're scared. I am, too. But I genuinely believe that we will be fine, that we'll be happier if we walk away," James said, trying to reassure her.

"Walking away from Callum doesn't scare me, James," she said, a high, shrill laugh following her words.

He sent her a sharp look. "Then what does, my dear?"

"Your reaction to what I'm about to tell you. Sit down, darling. You're not the only one who has a bombshell to drop."

Jules spent two hours enduring pitying looks, drinking one too many wine spritzers and batting off too many men looking for company.

How dare Garrett Kaye stand her up? Jules paid the taxi driver and stepped onto the sidewalk outside Garrett's building, watching the taxi pull back into the traffic. She'd have to call for another one later as she'd left her car in the parking garage because a) she'd had too many wine spritzers and b) she was mad, and it was her rule that a person shouldn't drink and drive or drive and fume.

Jules tipped her head back to look up at the sleek facade of Garrett's building. She counted the floors—eleven—and lights blazed from the tenth and eleventh stories. Prior to deciding to ask for his help, she'd researched him, annoyed at how little information she could find on the internet. But she did discover he lived in a luxurious penthouse apartment on the top floor of the building and that his office was one floor down. His employees' offices were another floor below, and he rented out the rest of the space to a prominent law firm.

Jules bit her bottom lip and jammed her hands into the pockets of her coat. It was late and she was a little buzzed, but she had to see him, now, *tonight*. She hated asking anyone for help—that wasn't what she did—but she didn't know where else to turn, what to do.

Kate was in a bad, bad way, racked with debt and floundering. When they'd spoken earlier in the day, Jules offered up savings, a not inconsiderable amount, but Kate, after thanking her profusely, refused her offer, telling her that her half a million wouldn't make a jot of difference. She owed tens of millions, and she was going to lose her business, all her properties and, horribly, the ranch.

She'd be left with nothing.

Jules immediately told Kate she could live with

her, that she'd support her...well, forever, if she had to. Kate had been Jules's port in a very violent storm, and Jules had no idea what she would've done without her. Kate had also launched Jules's career, and she basically owed her everything.

But she couldn't stand by and watch Kate sink, see the ranch that had been in Kate's family for generations pass into a stranger's hands. She had to do all she could to find the miracle Kate needed.

Garrett Kaye wasn't in the miracle business, but he dealt with ailing companies all the time, and maybe he knew—wunderkind that he was supposed to be—something no one else did. Maybe he could give her some advice on something, *anything*, Kate could do. Oh, she knew there was little chance of the business being saved, but maybe Garrett had an idea of how she could save the ranch.

She didn't have anyone else to whom she could turn. Her best friends were dealing with their family issues. Callum was still in the hospital after suffering a massive heart attack and was fighting off an infection after undergoing a triple bypass. Tinsley and Kinga were both helping James manage the family's massive international company, and her friends didn't have any experience dealing with a failing business. She only knew one person who did: Garrett.

She hadn't wanted to call him—she felt completely out of her depth with the man—but she'd walk through the flames of hell for Kate. She'd mustered the courage to text him, and he'd agreed to meet, but then the blasted man had stood her up.

Jerk.

But he was a jerk whose brain she needed to pick so here she was, determined to ask her questions, to interrupt whatever he was doing. God, she hoped he didn't have a woman up there. That would be awkward.

Awkward be damned. Kate's financial and emotional well-being were more important than Kaye's sex life. In Jules's mind, at least.

Jules walked to the main doors of the building and wasn't surprised to find them locked. She stepped over to a discreet door to the side but couldn't see an intercom. There was no way to call up to ask the occupant to let her up.

Dammit.

Good thing she had his number. Jerking her phone out of her bag, she found his contact details and tapped her foot as she waited for him to answer. And waited some more.

"Jules, hell, sorry, something came up."

"Apologize to my face, Kaye," Jules told him. "I'm outside your door. Let me in."

"Listen, it's not a good—"

"I waited two hours for you to show, Kaye," Jules interrupted him, her voice dripping acid. "Let. Me. In."

Jules heard Garrett's muttered curse, but the door clicked open. She stepped inside and realized she was in a private elevator. After the door shut behind her, the elevator whizzed her up with dizzying speed.

Seconds later the door opened to reveal a dark hallway. Jules dropped her bag to the floor and slowly unwound her scarf, her attention caught by the massive, abstract oil painting taking up most of the wall. She shrugged off her coat and, unable to find a coat hook, draped it over the arm of a chair in the corner, her head cocking as Tchaikovsky's *Sixth Symphony* washed over her, bleak and beautiful.

She recognized it immediately. Her mom—a talented musician—used to play Tchaikovsky on an old LP player after fighting with her dad. Growing up, Jules had heard this symphony, a terrifyingly sad piece of music, more often than a young child should.

Knowing that Garrett wouldn't hear her call his name over the sound of the alternating notes between the first and second violins, she walked into a large mostly empty great room. His penthouse apartment covered the entire top floor, and this room was situated in the corner of the building. Arched windows reflected the lights from the neighboring buildings and the harbor below. The space echoed the mood of the music. It was austere and a little desolate, with just a freestanding island with a marble top, a sleek dining table in front of the rectangular window in the corner and a long, low couch in front of the far wall to break up the vast space.

His apartment went beyond minimalist to stark. And cold. Jules shivered as the music turned ferocious, the sound of the snarling horns filling his space. Wishing she could switch it off, she looked around and saw Garrett next to the last window, his forearm resting against the glass above his head, watching the activity in the harbor.

As the instruments dropped out of the symphony, Jules wondered why Garrett was listening to such an emotive piece, what prompted him to choose the hauntingly sad symphony to accompany his thoughts.

"It's not a good time, Juliana-Jaliyah," Garrett told her, his voice a low growl in the sudden silence of the apartment.

He held a half-empty whiskey bottle in his right hand, and Jules stared at his hard profile, debating whether to leave.

"Interesting choice of music, Kaye. I never would've pegged you as someone who loved the classics," Jules stated.

"I love all music, classics included," Garrett said, without turning around. "It's said that Tchaikovsky wrote that piece as an elaborate suicide note."

"Because he was dead nine days after conducting the premiere, struck down by cholera he caught from drinking contaminated water." A sudden thought horrified her: he wasn't contemplating harming himself, was he? He didn't strike her as being depressed, but she needed to check. "Are you planning on drinking water contaminated by cholera, Kaye?"

She heard his hard snort and was immediately reassured. He looked like he had the weight of the world on his shoulders, but Jules knew he could handle whatever came his way. Even so, he looked very alone.

Jules walked across the vast space and stopped next to him. Taking a chance, she placed her hand in the center of his back and rested her head against his bicep. He'd either talk or he wouldn't, but for as long as he tolerated her presence, she'd stand here, giving him any comfort she could.

She felt his tension and watched as he lifted the whiskey bottle to his lips and took a long sip. A memory from her childhood slapped at her—bourbon instead of whiskey—and she tensed. How long had he been drinking, and how drunk was he? She was alone in his apartment, in this building, with a man she didn't know, a man with a bottle in his hand, someone who was upset.

Maybe she *should* leave…

"I'm not drunk, and I'd never hurt you," Garrett told her, in a clear, calm voice.

Jules stepped back and tipped her head to look at him. In the low light she saw that his eyes were clear.

He lifted his whiskey bottle. "I've only just opened this, and that was only my second belt."

He had a way of looking inside her and reading her, and it unsettled her. "How do you do that?" she asked him, genuinely curious. "How do you know what I'm feeling?"

He shrugged, turned, walked to the sleek dining table and banged the whiskey bottle on its surface. "You have the most expressive eyes—and face—of anyone I've ever met. And when I took a sip of whiskey, your entire body tensed."

So observant, even while upset.

Garrett picked up a tablet, hit a button and a series of lights came on, making Jules blink. Yep, his apartment was starker than she'd thought, dominated by white walls and those awesome windows. There was a basin and sleek cooker buried in the island but she couldn't see any appliances, cupboards or anything that hinted at a kitchen. How the hell did he cook?

Jules turned her attention back to Garrett. He looked...well, not awful—he was too good-looking for that—but like he'd had a day hand-delivered from hell. Blue stripes ran under his deep-set eyes, and his mouth was tight with tension. He still wore his suit, a deep navy and designer, but his tie was pulled loose, and his wavy hair looked messier than usual.

"Want something to drink?" Garrett asked her. He gestured to the whiskey bottle. "I have fifteen-year-old Scotch, but if you want something special, I have a full range of spirits and mixes as well."

Jules looked around for a drinks stand, or a cupboard that could hide a bar, but didn't see anything. His stash of liquor was probably hidden in his yet-to-be-revealed kitchen. Jules shook her head. "I already had a couple of drinks, while I waited for you."

Garrett stared at her, frowning, and then he winced. "Shit, I stood you up."

"You did," Jules agreed.

Garrett dropped an f-bomb and slapped his hands on his hips. As if only just realizing that he was still wearing his suit jacket, he pulled it off and threw it onto the couch. His tie followed its arc, and then he rolled up his sleeves. "I'm sorry. I should've let you know that I couldn't make it. That was rude of me."

It was. But Jules now suspected he had an incredibly good reason for standing her up. Walking over to the piano, she sat down on the stool and draped one leg over the other. "You offered me a drink, but I'd prefer coffee. Any chance of a cup?" She turned and looked at the marble island and lifted her eyebrows. "That is, if you have a machine. Or even a kettle."

Garrett stared at her for a long minute before nodding abruptly. He picked up his tablet and hit another button, and the far wall behind the marble island slid away, disappearing behind another wall. Jules blinked at the sleek kitchen in front of her, complete with high-end appliances and a coffee machine complicated enough to power a spaceship.

The disappearing wall also revealed a hallway. "What's beyond the kitchen?" Jules asked, fascinated by his high-tech, low-on-stuff apartment.

Garrett walked across the living area to his coffee machine. "Guest bedroom, my gym, a home study. Sauna and Jacuzzi." He hit a switch on the coffee machine, and the thing lit up like a UFO. "What do you want? Latte, cappuccino, espresso?"

His machine-gun questions amused her. "Black is fine."

"Jamaican, Kenyan, Colombian?"

Oh, God, the man was a coffee snob. "Surprise me," she told him. She looked around, eyebrows rising at the massive black-and-white painting on the far wall. "I presume the master suite is behind that sliding wall?"

"No sliding wall," Garrett told her, pulling levers on his machine. "Just a hidden door." He smiled, but Jules noticed that it was forced. "Why? Are you angling to see it?"

"In your dreams, Kaye," Jules tartly responded.

"Actually, you have been," Garrett muttered. Really? Had he been thinking about her, like that? She'd imagined she was the only one indulging in late-night, X-rated, naked-together fantasies.

He pulled her cup from the machine, placed it on a saucer and carried it over to her, pushing it into her hand. "The beans are from Sri Lanka... Tell me what you think."

Jules lifted the cup and hesitated. She frowned at him. "They had better not be the beans that have passed through the digestive tract of some primate, Kaye."

This time, Garrett's smile almost reached his eyes. "Not this time, Juliana. But if you are feeling adventurous..."

Jules scowled at him. "I will never feel that adventurous."

"Pity, because the coffee made from those beans are what angels drink in heaven," Garrett told her.

Jules took a sip of her coffee, sighed at the rich, complex taste and shifted in her seat. Her hand wobbled, and the coffee sloshed in the cup. Garrett quickly pulled the cup and saucer out of her hand.

"Hey!" she protested.

"That's a Fazioli, a limited-edition piano," Garrett told her, holding out his hand to her. "I don't know how clumsy you are, so let's move you, and your coffee, away from it."

"I'm not clumsy at all," Jules told him as he led her across the room to the long, uncomfortable-looking sofa. "I juggle bottles of expensive liquor for a living, and my clients don't like me breaking their bottles or their glasses. And it makes me look like an amateur."

His hand was warm and broad, and hers felt like it belonged there. And wasn't that one of the more stupid thoughts she'd had lately? Garrett Kaye wasn't for her. Nobody was. She'd never allow a man to get close enough to hurt her.

But when Garrett's thumb skimmed the skin above her thumb, she felt a bolt of pleasure slam through her, and she stumbled.

Garrett's mouth kicked up, mocking her previous statement. Jules didn't know whether she wanted to smack him or kiss him.

"You are very annoying," Jules told him, sitting down on the cold gray couch. But when she hit the cushions, she realized it was spectacularly comfortable. Garrett placed her coffee on the wood-and-steel coffee table and sat down next to her, resting his forearms on his knees, his hands dangling.

He'd made an effort to be hospitable, but she'd noticed the storms in his eyes, the tension in his shoulders. He looked like a man who needed a friend, someone to talk to. Didn't everybody, even reticent, arrogant billionaires, need a sounding board occasionally?

"Do you play?" Jules asked, gesturing to the piano.

"Yeah."

Right, she was going to have to pull some teeth to get him to open up. Jules took another sip of coffee, wondering why she felt compelled to dig a little deeper, to scratch away some of his layers. Maybe it was because his eyes were dark and turbulent. Maybe it was because his shoulders were halfway to his ears. Maybe it was because she was curious.

No matter the reason, she was going to dig.

"When I walked in, you were standing in the dark, looking like you were carrying the world and its baggage on your shoulders," Jules said, keeping her voice low. "And, annoying as you can be, I don't think you make a habit of standing women up, so something must've happened to upset you."

Embarrassment flashed across his face. "Sorry. Again."

"I wasn't looking for another apology, Garrett," Jules replied. She placed her hand on his thigh, sighing at his strength and heat. What would it be like to be surrounded by both?

Pulling her hand back, she lifted her coffee cup, surprised by the fine tremor in her hand. "I just wanted you to know that you can talk to me…if you want to." She shrugged, tried to smile. "And I'm a bartender, and whatever you say will be treated in the strictest confidence."

"Yeah, I don't think so," Garrett said, his voice rough.

His response wasn't a surprise. From the moment she met the man, she knew he was emotionally unavailable, someone who didn't open up easily. Or at all. Abrupt, direct, unemotional, he was the type of man she usually avoided. But yet here she sat, completely fascinated by him.

Jules put her cup on the table, folded her arms and gave the inside of her arm a hard pinch. Her objective was to help Kate, and help Kate was what she'd do.

And if that meant dancing with this devil, she'd do that, too.

Four

Her scent—light and lovely—was driving him mad. Because the urge to kiss her was nearly overwhelming, Garrett stood up and walked over to the window, leaning his shoulder into the cold pane. He eyed the whiskey bottle on the island, considered taking another drink and shrugged the urge away. His drinking made Jules tense up, and until he knew why it made her uncomfortable, he'd abstain.

Garrett looked at her, sitting there in her cranberry minidress that ended a couple of inches below her butt. His heart flipped over, and his stomach did a long roll as his eyes skimmed her curves. Below the hem of her dress, her solid black tights showed off her shapely thighs before disappearing into a pair of knee-high boots.

Her hair tumbled to her shoulders and down her back, and through her makeup, he could see the entrancing spray of freckles across her nose and over her cheeks. He wanted to play connect the dots, to see how far down her body those lovely spots went.

He wanted her, wanted to lose himself in her, in her slim body and delicious scent. He wanted to kiss that wide mouth and allow her taste to whirl him away from reality…

He wanted to forget, just for a little while, the conversation he'd had with James Ryder-White a few hours before, wanted to ignore James's request and his absurd statement that there was a good chance that Garrett would one day inherit a vast fortune.

That he was, by birth, a Ryder-White.

But Callum wasn't his father. James was.

Garrett still couldn't process the news, wasn't able to make sense of the bombshell James had dropped. He was his father, James stated, and he needed Garrett to manage the international empire. Hell, if he chose to let the world know he was James's firstborn, everything James would inherit—the Ryder International shares, the properties, Callum's wealth— would all pass to him. It was, James told him, a risk he was willing to take.

Ryder International needed an experienced CEO at the helm, and James wanted to get to know his son.

What. The. Hell?

The rumble in Garrett's stomach pulled him back to the present, and he couldn't remember when last he ate. And if Jules had been waiting for him for two hours, then she had to be hungry, too. And maybe after some food, he could start thinking properly, *unemotionally*.

"Have you eaten tonight?" he demanded, internally wincing at his terse tone.

"No, not yet."

"What if we ordered takeout, and while we're waiting, you tell me why you wanted to see me tonight?"

Jules stared at him, as if he were the spider and she the fly. After a tense thirty seconds, she finally nodded. "Okay."

Relief washed over him, as sweet as a soft spring morning. "What do you feel like eating?" he asked, pulling his phone out of the back pocket of his pants. "Pizza? Chinese? Indian? I eat everything, so you choose."

"There's a low-key but fantastic Korean place a few blocks north of here, The Homesick Korean. Do you know it?"

He shook his head. "I don't."

Jules got up and walked toward his hallway, and Garrett sucked in a harsh breath, wondering if she'd changed her mind and was leaving. When she returned holding her phone to her ear, his heart settled.

"Have you eaten Korean food before?" Jules asked. When he shook his head, she nodded and spoke into the phone and ordered a range of dishes in what sounded to him like passable Korean. After giving his address, she disconnected and tossed her phone on the couch.

"Do you speak Korean?"

Her smile finally hit her eyes. "Just enough to order."

Garrett followed her to the couch and sat down, keeping a broad cushion between them. Why tempt himself? "What are we eating?"

"Sweet and sour pork, spicy seafood mix served with udon noodles, and seafood and spring onion pancakes."

"Sounds good," Garrett commented. He rested his arm along the back of the sofa, his fingers very close to her sweet-smelling, bouncy hair. God, he loved her loose, natural curls, her exquisite profile, the way her dress flowed over her breasts.

"Tell me why you wanted to see me tonight," Garrett said on a long sigh. It would be at least twenty minutes before their food arrived, and he needed something to think about other than what she looked like naked.

Jules turned to face him and gestured to her boots. "Do you mind if I get comfortable?"

Garrett shook his head and watched as Jules slid down the zip on the backs of her boots and pulled them off. She wiggled her toes, sighed and then rotated her feet, groaning a little.

All his blood went south at hearing that little sound. Would she sound as breathless when he slid inside her?

"That feels so much better," Jules said. She tucked her feet under her bottom and turned to him, her face serious.

"I need your help," she baldly stated.

That was the second time he'd heard that phrase tonight. People never asked him for help, but today, in the space of four hours, he'd had the same request twice. Since he doubted that Jules was about to ask him to run a multibillion dollar company, he told himself to relax.

Garrett gestured for her to keep talking.

"At the Valentine's Day Ball, I told you about Kate Kennedy, the owner of Crazy Kate's."

Yeah, he remembered.

Despair dropped into Jules's eyes and pulled her wide mouth down. "She's about to lose everything, Garrett. Her house in Denver, her business, her assets. And her beloved ranch."

Judging by the wobble of her bottom lip, the possibility of losing Kate's ranch was eating Jules alive. He waited for her to explain, and when she just stared at her toes, he placed a hand on her foot and squeezed. "I'm sorry to hear that, Jules, but I'm not sure how I can help."

When Jules looked at him, her eyes were large and sad, green instead of gold. "I need you to look at her business, find a way for her to keep it going."

Garrett stared at her, wincing again. He knew that there was no chance of that happening. What Kate needed was someone with deep pockets, a person who didn't care when he'd see a return on his investment, someone who didn't care if he ever saw a profit.

Those sorts of suckers were few and far between.

"Honey, I've been keeping an eye on the company, and I think Crazy Kate's is beyond help," he told her, trying to be as gentle as he could.

Jules's curls bounced as she shook her head. "I refuse to believe that. Surely something can be saved? She doesn't have to lose everything!"

"She's mortgaged every property she owns, and the bank needs a way to recoup some of those losses."

"The ranch is her home, dammit! Kilconnell Ranch has been in her family for six generations. She's emotionally attached to that land."

And so are you. "It's really bad business to mortgage a property you love and never want to lose."

"I know that, but desperate people do desperate things." Jules rubbed her forehead with her fingers. "Everybody has written her off. Everybody wants her to fail. I just want someone to go and talk to her, look at her business and her books and see if there's a way to get her to succeed. Or if not succeed, to help her keep her ranch."

Jules was tilting her sword at a windmill, and she was going to stab herself in the foot. Or in the heart. "Banks don't want businesses to fail, Jules. Foreclosing isn't good for business, and if she's that deep in debt, they'll probably also take a hit."

"So you're telling me to accept it?" Jules demanded, her expression suggesting that he'd asked her to kick a kitten.

"I'm trying to be realistic, Juliana. Giving you false hope won't do anyone any good."

Jules stared down at his hand still holding her foot. "I just need to do anything I can, Garrett."

Her compulsion to help her friend touched him, and he sighed, knowing that he might regret his next words. "What, exactly, do you want from me, Jules?"

Jules pushed an agitated hand through her hair. "Would you consider coming to Denver with me this weekend? I'd like you to talk to Kate, look at her books and try to find something, anything, to help her save the business."

Garrett stared at her, trying to make sense of her words. "You're asking me to fly to Denver to look at someone's business, hoping that I will be able to save it?" he clarified.

Jules nodded. "Even if you can just find a way to save the ranch, I'd be grateful."

He looked into her astounding eyes and found himself on the point of saying yes, of agreeing to her absurd proposal. He shook his head, trying to harden his heart.

He was the owner of a massive company. He had far more important projects demanding his attention. He needed to wrap his head around his parentage and James's offer for him to take on the CEO position at Ryder International.

Even if Garrett had some spare time and the emotional energy to help her out, there wasn't anything he could do.

"Garrett, you're her only chance!"

That was where she was wrong: not even he could rescue Crazy Kate's and the ranch. Well, he could, by throwing fifty million at the problem—fifty million he'd never recoup. He was a businessman, not a philanthropist.

Garrett pulled in a deep breath and looked for his patience. It was a commodity in short supply. He squeezed her foot and waited until she looked at him. "What do I do, Jules?"

Jules frowned at his question. "You buy struggling companies and either put them back on their feet or you buy them and strip them of their assets."

Close enough. "As I said, I've been keeping an eye on Crazy Kate's. I had my people research the company. If there was a chance the business could be rehabilitated, I would've looked into it some more, but it's too far gone, even for me."

Jules lifted her face, and her eyes collided with his, fierce and fantastic. "I wish that everyone would put as much effort into proving it viable as they do into believing it's not!"

This was why emotion and business were such bad bedfellows. "It isn't a matter of belief but of numbers. The numbers are goddamn awful, Jules."

And he, like others in this game, didn't believe in flogging dead horses. Or businesses.

"What does the ranch mean to you, Jules?" he asked, curious.

A rich cloud of emotions turned her eyes to gold, then to copper, to green and then back to gold. "The ranch is happiness, stability, security. Kate is, and always has been, my rock and my anchor, the one person I have always been able to rely on."

"Are you related to her?" Garrett asked.

The shake of her head told him that she wasn't. "But she's family, someone I *chose*, someone who chose *me*. I travel a lot, Garrett. I'm never in one place for long, and I like it that way. It suits me. I have an efficiency apartment, a place where I can dump my stuff. But Kilconnell Ranch is my *home*. And the thought of anyone else but Kate living there is driving me crazy."

And making her sad. And he'd do anything not to make her sad.

"Okay."

Jesus, what? Had he just said yes to visiting the ranch?

Garrett, wondering what alien had invaded his brain, turned his head to look outside, seeing the wet streets of Portland, the heavy clouds blotting out the stars. If he stayed in the city for the weekend, he'd spend most of his time in his office one floor down, working and brooding, fixating on his parentage and digesting James's news. He tasted anger in the back of his throat and knew it was coated with bitter hurt.

Thanks to his mother's stubbornness, he'd been fatherless for thirty-five years. And it didn't escape his notice that James had only come clean when he needed help. It wasn't about what Garrett needed. His mother had put her career above his need for a father; James needed Garrett's business expertise to steer Ryder International through rocky waters. His parents, such as they were, only looked after them-selves and their interests.

And it made him goddamn furious.

James had suggested getting together this week-end, but Garrett wasn't ready to see him again, didn't know if he ever would be. So maybe it was better that he did leave town, that he put a little distance between the situation and his turbulent emotions. He could go to Colorado with Jules, paw through Kate's papers and set her mind at ease that there wasn't any-thing anyone could do.

He'd breathe the mountain air, maybe take a hike—when was the last time he had spent any time in nature or even outdoors?—and figure out what he wanted from the Ryder-White family.

If he wanted anything at all.

One of the perks of being wealthy was owning a plane, and Garrett loved the freedom it gave him. Twelve hours after agreeing to accompany Jules to Colorado, he was winging his way west, Jules sitting in the enormous leather chair opposite him looking excited and happy.

His pilot announced they were starting their de-scent to Durango-La Plata County Airport, and Gar-rett asked Jules to fasten her seat belt. She sent him a quick smile, her eyes shining with eagerness. And hope.

"I can't wait to get to the ranch, to see Kate," she told him, not for the first time. "As soon as you get there, you'll understand why I—we—love the place so much and why we think it's worth saving.

"It's a sunshiny place, especially in summer, and

the wildflowers in spring are brilliant. It's an alpine paradise, with these incredible views of the mountains. The wildlife is incredible and there's an alpine lake stocked with brown trout. It's right next door to a national forest so there's a lot of land to explore…" Jules nibbled on her bottom lip, and Garrett thought he saw the sheen of tears in her fantastically expressive eyes. "God, I sound like a tour guide… It's worth saving, Garrett," she quietly added.

He'd done his research on the property. With its stone-and-wood mansion and extensive outbuildings, the ranch sounded amazing but, unfortunately, banks and lending institutions didn't care about amazing vistas and alpine lakes. They dealt in certainties and cash, both of which were in noticeably short supply.

"Thank you for doing this, Garrett. I am so grateful." She placed a hand on her heart and tapped her fingers against her chest. "I know you will find something to help save the ranch."

Hope flared in her eyes, and her complete confidence in his abilities made him feel ten feet tall, like he could jump mountains and swim oceans. She looked at him like he'd hung the moon and stars. Nobody had ever, ever looked at him like that before.

This was why men did stupid things for women, he decided. Why they bought flowers, wore cologne, kept their cars clean… Just to see a woman looking at him like this.

Garrett knew she was about to launch herself into his arms, but if she did that, he'd be French-kissing her in two seconds, and she'd be naked in three.

Get a grip, Kaye. You know how this is going to end, so be an adult and prepare her for disappointment.

He held up his hand and frowned, trying to tamp down her enthusiasm. He needed to bring her back down to planet earth because he was certain looking at Kate's financials would confirm what he already knew. "Jules, this is a long shot. There is a less-than-zero-percent chance of me finding anything that can help her. You know this, right?"

Her pretty nose wrinkled, and irritation flashed in her eyes.

"I'm not going to lie to you. Or give you false hope," Garrett warned her. "I know how much you want a miracle, but I'm not in the miracle business."

"I get it," Jules said, all but bouncing in her seat.

Garrett gripped the bridge of his nose with his thumb and index finger. He lowered her hand and scowled at her. "I don't think you do," he growled. "There's a really good chance that her business troubles will be worse than you expected."

A little of her excitement dimmed. "I just want someone to look at it from another angle," she muttered.

This was such a goddamn waste of time. Why had he agreed to this madness? Oh, right, because she looked so damn sad. He was such a sap.

Garrett closed his eyes and shook his head. This wasn't going to end well. He could feel it in his bones. He might be selfish, but the best he could hope for from this weekend was that the quiet and the sweet mountain air, and being out of Portland, would help him to decide whether he was going to, on a very temporary basis, run Ryder International.

He should say no, keep his distance... He was in his midthirties; he didn't need to be part of a god-damn family. He didn't need Callum's inheritance or the burden of Ryder International, and if he kept his father's identity to himself—James promised that he would respect his wishes in that regard—his life needn't change at all.

James, as per Callum's instruction, would find another CEO and would inherit the company and Callum's assets. That was fair and right. James was, after all, the next in line.

But James told him, with unexpected candor and sincerity, that he wasn't interested in his inheritance. He'd far rather have a relationship with his firstborn and pass Ryder International to the next generation. James's only proviso was that it was an all-or-nothing situation. Garrett had to be all in or all out; there was no in-between. While James wasn't asking him to change his name—not that he would—Garrett couldn't pick and choose how he wanted to be in-volved with the famous family.

All in. Or all out. It was a helluva decision to make.

"You have that same look on your face as you did last night," Jules commented.

Garrett's eyes slammed into hers. "What do you mean?"

"Now and again, when you think I'm not paying attention, you look a little sad, a lot lost and very confused," Jules explained. She cocked her head and her eyes drilled into him. "What happened yesterday, Garrett?"

He wasn't going to tell her. He couldn't.

"James Ryder-White came to see me yesterday, a few hours before you did. He was my last meeting of the day." Garrett heard the words tumble from his lips and cursed himself. Why the hell was he telling her this? This was super classified information, and if it got out, the share prices of both Kaye Capital and Ryder International would dip, rise and swirl around.

Jules narrowed her eyes at him, her mind obviously going a mile a minute. "What did he come to see you about? As far as I can tell, you have nothing in common. You are different ages, different industries, and, judging by your tense, quick conversation at the Valentine's Day Ball, you aren't friends. So what did he want with you?"

He didn't answer her question. Not that she expected him to.

They were in a holding pattern, high above the airport, waiting to land, and if Jules didn't get Garrett talking now, she never would. Jules tapped her finger on her thigh, wondering how to get him to talk. He'd told her, more than a few times, that there was no chance of him finding any solution to Kate's horrible dilemma, so she couldn't help wondering why he'd decided to accompany her to Colorado, why he was using his considerable resources on what he kept saying was a wild-goose chase. If the chase was so wild, and the goose so elusive, why was he here, with her?

No, there had to be another reason why he was flying west with her. And it had something to do with James Ryder-White. She thought she'd try another question but didn't expect to get anywhere. "If you think that there's no hope for Kate, why are you here? With me?"

"As you said, if anyone can find a solution, it'll be me. But I don't want you getting your hopes up and then blaming me when it comes to nothing."

Nope, not buying that. "Then why do I feel like you are running away from Portland, Garrett? And what does it have to do with James Ryder-White?"

"I don't run. From anything," Garrett told her, sounding annoyed.

Jules fought the urge to roll her eyes. "Okay. Then why are you wanting to put some distance between you and James?"

Garrett ran both hands over his face, dropping them to glare at her. "You're going to keep nagging me for an answer, aren't you?"

"Probably," Jules cheerfully replied.

"Shit. Well, this is classified information, so if you blab, I'll know it came from you."

Jules nodded and waved his words away.

"Callum Ryder-White recently had a triple heart bypass and is still in hospital fighting an infection."

"I know. Tinsley and Kinga are my closest friends."

He glared at her. "Did you know that Callum

asked James to find a temporary CEO to run Ryder International while he was incapacitated?"

No, that was news. "James has worked for Callum all his life. Surely he can run the organization?" Jules asked.

"You'd think," Garrett snapped. "But no, Callum doesn't think James has enough of a killer instinct. He instructed James to find someone to run the organization."

A bank load of pennies dropped. Jules gasped. "You?"

"Me," Garrett confirmed.

Jules frowned, puzzled. James's request made absolutely no sense. Garrett had no connection to Ryder International—okay, his mother had held the position as Callum's personal assistant forever, but Garrett and Callum had no business ties or shared business interests.

"Why you?" Jules demanded.

He opened his mouth to answer her but then turned away to look out the window to the ground below. Right, so he knew the reason why James approached him but wasn't ready to share that with her yet.

Silly to feel so hurt, but she did.

Jules stared at his broad chest, noticing the way it tapered down to his waist. He had a great chest, with wide shoulders, and his legs were long and muscled. He really was the most masculine guy she'd ever met, an intriguing combination of power and grace.

"Why me?" Garrett repeated her question, handing her a self-mocking smile. "Well, I do have an MBA and am one of the most successful venture capitalists in the country."

Probably in the world and the galaxy. Jules released an annoyed puff of air. "We both know you can do the job, Kaye! But why did James ask you? Especially since you are known to be a workaholic and have a revolving door of projects."

"Have you been researching me, Juliana-Jaliyah?"

"Stop trying to provoke me, and answer the damn question," Jules snapped. "And if you don't want to tell me why, then just say so."

"I don't want to tell you," Garrett replied. "It's personal…and I'm still wrapping my head around all that he said."

Annoyance and hurt rolled over her, and Jules nodded. The man, she reluctantly conceded, was entitled to his secrets. She barely knew him, so she couldn't expect him to confide in her. But she wanted him to. She wanted him to trust her and to talk to her. She wanted to peel back his layers and see who he was beneath the cool composure.

But that wasn't in the cards…

Jules played with her seat-belt buckle and forced her mouth up into an impersonal smile. She heard the sound of the engines changing, knew they were descending and looked out the window onto a clear but cold late winter's day in Colorado. This weekend might be the last weekend she spent at Kilconnell Ranch, and she wouldn't let Garrett's terse and uncommunicative manner taint her memories. She'd laugh with Kate and Peta, take a horse for a ride, stare at the mountains and take a thousand mental snapshots.

And pray that Garrett would find something, anything, to save the only home she'd ever known.

Five

Storm clouds chased them from the airport in Durango to Silverton, where they stopped for coffee. The town was busy with tourists who'd come to enjoy the March snow. They didn't linger to explore the town—filled with boutiques, shops and restaurants—and were soon on the road to Kilconnell Ranch, a half-hour drive away.

Garrett handled the SUV he'd rented with cool competence, tackling the curvy road with confidence. Happy to let him drive, Jules sat back in her seat and watched the passing scenery, marveling at the views of the majestic peaks, picking out familiar landmarks as the vehicle flew down the road.

It was a wild, desolate, primal area, but she loved it for being untouched, lovely and fierce. And as she always did when she traveled this road, she felt like she was on her way home and would soon be stepping into a house filled with love.

Talking about love...

"So Kate lives with her wife, Peta. They've been together for many years and married two years ago." She darted a look at Garrett's profile. He was gorgeous and hot and ripped, but if he was intolerant, it was going to be a very long two days.

The edges of his mouth lifted. "I don't give a rat's ass how people love each other, Jules. None of my business."

Thank God.

"We'll be there in about fifteen minutes. You'll be sleeping in the guest suite in the east wing. It has amazing views of the mountains," Jules informed him.

"And where will you be sleeping, Juliana?" Garrett asked, his voice silky.

"Not with you," she quickly responded.

"Pity."

Jules stared out the window, wanting to tell him that, while she dumped her clothes and toiletries in the attic bedroom, she never slept upstairs, preferring to sleep on the couch in front of the fire or on the sofa in the study. He'd think her weird if she told him she used bedrooms as a place to store clothes, to dress and put on makeup, but that she hadn't slept in a bed since she was six or seven.

She could lie in a bed and read but she couldn't fall asleep in one and found bedrooms claustrophobic and confining. And yeah, her aversion was why she hadn't managed to have sex yet.

That meant going without sex, and that totally sucked. But she couldn't tell anyone about her phobia, didn't know how to explain that sleeping in a room with a bed—or the thought of making love to a man in there—made her want to hyperventilate.

Thanks, Dad.

"I want you, Jules. You know that."

Actually, he'd been thinking about little else since he'd met her. He kept imagining her lithe body naked, the color of her nipples, whether she waxed or was au naturel. He didn't have a preference: it was her body, and it would be a privilege to enjoy it however she presented herself. And yeah, he wasn't going to lie to himself, a part of his reasoning for accepting her invitation to accompany her to Colorado was to see if they could take their chemistry up a notch, to share her bed. She was such a curious, wonderful combination of sarcasm and strength. She was tempting and tantalizing and, yes, trouble.

He liked sex, was good at it, but Jules was the only woman who'd caught his eye in over three months, maybe four.

He wanted sex, but more than that, he wanted sex with *her*.

"You make it sound so easy, so rational," Jules said, and Garrett heard the tremor in her voice. "So damn natural."

"It is natural," he stated, confidently steering into a sharp bend.

"To someone who's had a lot of it, I suppose it is," Jules mused. "I haven't had enough of it to know."

Garrett frowned. Did she really think he would judge her for not being experienced?

"There's nothing wrong with not having had many lovers," Garrett quietly stated.

"Or any at all."

It took him a minute to understand what she was trying to say. He swallowed, then swallowed again. She was a virgin? No, he had to have misunderstood her. "You've never…?"

He looked at her, caught the flash of green before she spoke again. "I'm not completely inexperienced but…I've never had penetrative sex. God, this is embarrassing."

It shouldn't be. "I don't believe in slut-shaming women. If guys can enjoy sex, so can women. Fair is fair," he stated. "Conversely, I would never judge anyone for staying celibate, for being choosy. I believe in personal choice."

He saw her shoulders drop an inch and some of the tension leave her face. He returned his attention to the road, his brow furrowed in thought. How the hell was she still a virgin? She was in her late twenties. Surely there must've been someone who'd caught her fancy over the years? She was gorgeous and a minor celebrity; she had to have had offers.

She said that she wasn't inexperienced… But what the hell did that mean? Was she implying that she'd had oral sex? But that didn't make sense, either. Oral sex was as intimate, if not more intimate, than penetrative sex… Why would she have one and not the other?

His mind was spinning, and there was only one thought that stayed front and center.

He still wanted her more than he wanted to breathe. And it wasn't because he'd had weird news from James and was feeling off balance but because she was a sexy, smart, forthright woman, and being naked with her would be a pleasure. And a privilege.

"Do you think your virginity is something to be saved for marriage?"

"Not particularly," Jules replied.

Her short, snippy reply told him that she was done discussing the subject, but he wasn't. He still had a point to make. "To me, sex is natural, recreational, fun, something I do because I enjoy it and I'm good at it. Virgin or not, I want to make love to you…with you. It will be phenomenal."

"How do you know that?" Jules threw up her hands, and when she looked at him, he saw the flush on her cheeks and the embarrassment in her eyes. "You can't know that! We haven't even kissed yet!"

That was what she was worried about? Hell, he could fix that immediately. Garrett peered through the windshield, saw the turnoff to a logging road coming up and pulled into it. After making sure he was completely off the road, he hit the button to undo his seat belt and turned to face Jules, who looked at him with wide eyes.

"What the hell are you doing, Garrett?"

"Kissing you, Jules." Because her eyes held a hint of anxiety, he grinned at her. "Pucker up, princess."

Amusement pulled her lips upward. "You are ridiculous."

Garrett smiled at her as he lifted his hand to her soft cheek, his thumb brushing over her lovely cheekbone. "Let me show you just how much chemistry is arcing between us, Juliana."

He lowered his head to hers and butted his forehead against hers, keeping his touch gentle. He looked into her eyes—how could he not?—and then scanned her lovely face. Looking at her was such a pleasure and made his heart sigh, then sing. Needing to feel her skin, he used his thumb to graze the side of her face, exploring the skin below her ear. He moved his head slightly and used his cheekbone to connect with hers and rubbed their skin together, and when he heard her shaky breath, he knew she was as turned on as he was.

"Can I kiss you, sweetheart?" he murmured, needing to know.

Her yes was shaky but there, so he placed light kisses on her mouth, her jawline and her neck as his hand slid over her hip and flirted with the top of her ass. He came back to her lips, not afraid to linger a little. When her mouth parted and the hand on the back of his neck tightened, he slid his tongue between her teeth and...

Another big bang, greater and more intense than

the original boom that started life on earth, rocked him off his feet. Garrett found himself falling, coming apart, re-amalgamating in a way that he didn't recognize.

Her hand on his face scorched him, her tongue branded him and his mind dissolved and only contained one word...maybe two.

Mine.

More.

He was standing on a precipice, and if he allowed this to continue, he'd take her now, on the side of the road. And judging by the way she was kissing him back, she might just let him.

It took everything he had, every last ounce of willpower, to pull back, to rest his cheek against hers. They'd just kissed, yet he felt like he'd been ripped apart by a tornado, smacked by an avalanche.

"Wow," Jules murmured.

He pulled back to look at her. Her eyes were glassy with desire, and the pulse point in her neck was beating as fast as a hummingbird's wings. Oh, yeah, *chemistry* was too small a word to describe what was bubbling between them.

Jules stared at him, wide-eyed, and he dragged his thumb across her bottom lip, telling himself that he couldn't, shouldn't—mustn't—dive back in.

Because if he did, he wouldn't be able to stop. And their first time—because there would be a first time—would not take place in the front seat of a car.

She deserved a soft bed, fragrant-smelling sheets, a warm room. Everything that was magic.

At Kilconnell Ranch, Garrett followed Jules's instructions to park in the empty bay of the detached garage. On spotting Peta walking up from the stables, accompanied by a lone mixed-breed dog, Jules bounded out of the car. She ran to meet Peta, Kate's forewoman and wife, and wrapped her arms around the slim and wiry woman. Peta looked and smelled the same.

No, Jules thought when she pulled back to gaze into her old friend's face, maybe not quite the same. The wrinkles on the edges of her eyes and around her mouth were deeper, she looked thinner and her eyes were definitely worried.

Jules squeezed her again and placed her cheek against Peta's to whisper in her ear. "I'm trying to find a solution, Pete."

Peta patted her cheek. "I know you are," she replied, before turning to Garrett and holding out her hand and introducing herself.

Garrett, dressed in designer jeans, brand-new boots and a fancy jacket, dropped the luggage he was holding to shake Peta's hand. He rubbed his palms together. "Holy crap, it's cold."

"We're expecting a storm to roll in later," Peta told him. She glanced at her watch, looking worried. "Kate and I need to go into town, and if we want to get back before the conditions turn ugly, we've got to leave soon. Let's get you guys inside."

Jules followed Peta toward the wooden front door. Garrett walked next to her, carrying their overnight bags in one hand, his other hand low on her back. Her shoulder brushed his, and she felt like she belonged at his side. One kiss and she was having silly notions, ones that didn't have any basis in reality.

No matter how good a kisser he was, how many wildfires he ignited inside her, he wasn't for her. She couldn't cope with hard, reticent men dealing with demons. She had too many of her own to be able to take on someone else's.

"Where is Kate?" Jules asked, conscious of the heat of Garrett's body and big hand as they walked into the spacious hallway of the ranch house. A pack of dogs bolted out from their beds by the fire in the great room and swarmed them, shoving noses into hands and crotches, demanding attention.

Jules greeted them all, smiling when she saw Garrett on his haunches, enthusiastically handing out ear and tummy rubs. Being such a city boy, she was surprised to see how comfortable he was around dogs. She was stupidly attracted to the man, that much was obvious, but seeing him with the dogs upped her *like* factor.

The attraction she could deal with and ignore—kinda, sorta—but *like* was much more dangerous.

"Kate is trying to get all the documents in some sort of order for your man here," Peta told her. "She had an offer on the building, and she moved all the records from the plant in Denver to the ranch."

An offer on the building had to be good news and

Jules felt a spurt of excitement. "Did she get a decent price for the building?"

Peta shook her head. "Sale fell through."

Crap. Jules slumped and felt Garrett's big hand squeezing her shoulder, a quick, silent gesture of encouragement. She wasn't in this alone; he was here to help.

If he could. But as good as Garrett was, he wasn't a miracle worker, as he kept reminding her.

Jules walked into the great room with its huge, exposed beams and stone wall behind the oversize fireplace. Double-volume windows brought the outside in, and the view was all the artwork the room needed. Plump, inviting couches, bright cushions and a massive fire made the huge room seem cozy and homey. Jules, so in tune with this place, immediately noticed something missing. There were no animals in the fields. "Where are the animals, Pete?"

Peta turned oh-so-sad eyes on her. "We were offered a really good price for the herd, and a neighbor agreed to take the horses."

Jules felt tears sting her eyes. The ranch wasn't the ranch without animals milling around. The land felt desolate and empty. "Could you not keep them?"

"Animals cost money, Jules," Garrett told her, his deep voice rolling over her. "Selling them is a quick way to cut costs."

"You're not just a pretty face," Peta told him, in her blunt way of speaking. "Kate cried for a week after the animals were hauled away."

Jules didn't blame her. She felt like crying, too.

"Juliana!"

Jules spun around at the sound of Kate's voice, and she saw her second mom standing in the doorway to the great room, dressed only in a thin cashmere sweater and blue jeans. Jules ran to Kate, flinging her arms around her slim frame and rocking her from side to side.

"God, I missed you. I've been so worried about you," Jules told her when she finally let Kate go. She frowned at her drawn face and worried eyes. "Are you okay?"

Kate lifted a thinner-than-normal shoulder. "As good as anyone can be when facing becoming homeless."

"You and Peta will always have a home with me," Jules told her, squeezing her hands.

"Oh, there are places we can go, but this is home, this is our place," Kate told her, her eyes bright with tears. "This is where I was born, where we got married, where I want to die."

Jules hugged her and placed a kiss on her temple. "I know. That's why I brought Garrett along. He's brilliant, and hopefully he'll find a way to save the ranch."

"From your words to God's ears," Kate said. They both looked at Garrett, standing by the bank of windows with his back to them, taking in the breathtaking view of the mountains looming over the ranch. Jules called his name, and Garrett turned, smiled and headed toward them. Jules turned to look at Kate, saw her eyes widen and a small smile touch her mouth.

"My, my, he's a long, lovely drink of water." She smiled at Jules. "Are you two together?"

Jules rolled her eyes. "No, Kate. I asked him out here to help you!"

"Pity," Kate said, leaning against the eight-foot doorframe and watching Garrett.

"He's not my type, Kate," Jules said, her voice harder than usual.

Kate gave Garrett another up-and-down look. "Tall, big, muscular. What's not to like?"

She did like him, wanted to get naked with him, but she was still trying to convince herself that her attraction to him was an aberration, a step out of time. He wasn't anything like the guys she normally dated. She normally batted away the testosterone types and had drinks and dinner with guys who were gentle, sensitive, sometimes meek, always mild. They were, she realized, easy to handle and very easy to walk away from.

"Nothing can, or will, happen between us," Jules told Kate, keeping her voice low. Was she assuring Kate or herself?

After being introduced to Garrett, shaking his hand and exchanging small talk, Kate thanked him for his offer to help and explained that the Crazy Kate paperwork was in her study upstairs.

"I hope Jules hasn't oversold my expertise, Kate," Garrett told her, sliding his hands into the back pockets of his jeans. "I think the chances of my finding a solution are minimal, at best."

Kate nodded. "I appreciate you trying. There are also records on my computer. Don't feel shy about digging in."

"Kate, if you still want to go to town, we need to leave now," Peta told her.

Jules cast a questioning glance at Kate.

Kate rubbed her arm. "Frank fell and broke his hip, and Goldy brought him home this morning. I promised to take them some supplies as they are out of everything. And Peta says we need to get back before the storm hits."

Frank had worked as a ranch hand for thirty years and Goldy as Kate's housekeeper for almost as long. They'd retired to a small house on the outskirts of Silverton two years ago. Kate took her responsibilities to her people seriously—whether they were retired or not—and wouldn't be able to rest until she knew they had food in the fridge and were as comfortable as they could be.

"Send them my love," Jules told them.

"Will do," Kate said, taking her coat from Peta, who was looking impatient. Jules glanced at the patchy blue and cloudy sky. Experience told her not to dismiss Peta's gut. If she said a storm was rolling in, then it was.

"I've put Garrett in the east wing, Ju. There's stew and freshly baked bread for lunch. Help yourselves to anything else you need." Kate kissed Jules's cheek and sent Garrett a friendly smile. "Make yourself at home."

Garrett inclined his head. "Thank you."

Kate and Peta left the house, slamming the door behind them. Jules turned to Garrett and nodded to the stairs.

"Well, at least they stayed long enough for me to introduce you," Jules said.

"No worries. I don't need to be entertained," Garrett told her. He looked down at their bags, still lying in the middle of the hallway floor. "Shall I take these up?"

Jules used her foot to push them to the side. "We can take them with us when we go up. The house is enormous by the way. Kate and Peta's rooms are to the right of the staircase—they occupy the west wing. The guest bedrooms, including yours, are to the left of the stairs. Kate's study is in the center of the two wings, the door directly in front of you as you hit the top of the stairs. There's also a guest suite on the third floor. That's my space."

Garrett walked back into the great room, and Jules followed him. It looked, smelled and felt like home, somewhere she could breathe.

"It's a beautiful place," Garrett mused. "How big is the ranch?"

"Eight thousand or so acres," Jules immediately answered. "With two lakes and a river running through it, it has ample water. The house, as you can see, is stunning. There are three barns and another guesthouse."

Jules knew she sounded like a real estate agent, but she needed Garrett to understand that this property was worth saving, that he needed to find a way to save the land that had been in Kate's family for over a hundred years.

"I'm trying to be strong for them, upbeat and positive," Jules said, keeping her eyes on the highest peak in the distance. "But the thought of losing this property makes my throat burn and my heart weep."

Garrett walked across the room and through the door leading to a huge country kitchen. His voice floated back to her, asking her if she wanted coffee. When she stepped into the kitchen, she noticed that he'd found the coffee machine she'd bought Kate and Peta for Christmas two years ago.

"Where do they keep the mugs?"

"In the cupboard beneath the machine," Jules told him. She admired the way his jeans tightened to show his perfect butt as he bent down to open the cupboard door.

Garrett stood up, holding two huge mugs, one of which had been her favorite mug as a teenager.

"You are obviously attached to Kate and this property," Garrett said, checking the level of beans and water in the machine.

"I spent every summer holiday here since the time I was ten. For two months of the year, from the time I stepped out of the car to the moment Kate took me back to the city, my life made sense."

Garrett shoved the cup under the spout and tapped the side of his fist against the relevant button. It had taken her a year to figure out the intricacies of the machine, yet Garrett seemed to know exactly what to do. He was a coffee savant, she decided. Jules hoped he was also a save-the-ranch savant.

"But you're not related to her?" Garrett asked, whipping away a cup and repeating the process.

Jules stared past him to look out the bank of picture windows to the back pasture. In spring, it would be covered in wildflowers. God, she hoped she got to see it.

She felt Garrett's eyes on her face, knew he was waiting for her answer. How much to tell him? "There's a women's shelter in Denver. We happened to spend some time in it."

"*We* being who?" Garrett asked, his focus completely on her.

"My mom and I," Jules told him, pulling out a kitchen chair and sitting down at the long, rustic-chic table. "Before she went insolvent, Kate was seriously wealthy. She comes from old money. And her family were big-time philanthropists, but Kate gets... involved. She gets her hands dirty. She works in homeless shelters, volunteers at animal-rescue centers, shelters for women and children on the run."

The coffee machine hissed, but Garrett kept his eyes on her, his attention laser-sharp. He gestured for her to carry on talking.

"Kate was working at the shelter we found ourselves in, and we just clicked. And when my mom started feeling unsafe, terrified to stay in one place in case my abusive father found us, she told Kate we were going to leave. It was the end of spring, and Kate offered to take me home for the summer. Thanks to some fake identity documents Kate paid for, we remained in Denver, and the next summer I came back here. And all my vacations after that. This place became my second home."

She wasn't looking in his direction, but she felt his tension, knew his eyes had sharpened. She never spoke of her childhood and her father's abuse. It was a secret she never shared with anyone. Jules didn't understand why it felt so natural to explain a little of her sordid past to Garrett. But she couldn't sit still, so she jumped up and walked over to the window in the alcove adjoining the kitchen and rested her bottom on the windowsill, stretching out her legs.

"You said your mom was scared… Was your dad actively looking for you, or was your mom just being cautious?"

"Nope, he was tracking us," Jules told him, keeping her voice flat. Unable to look at him, she stood up and turned to look out of the window. The view always soothed her. "He nearly found us in Minneapolis, and in Wichita. Once we turned a corner and saw him standing on the doorstep to our apartment building. Another time a neighbor told us that he'd been around, inquiring after us."

"Jesus."

She heard Garrett's footsteps approaching and sighed when his arms slid around her waist, pulling her up so that she stood flush against him. He rested his chin in her hair. "Did he find you?"

"Not me, but he did find my mom. We heard, through someone back in Boston, that he was tired of tracking us, that we could stay gone as far as he was concerned. We decided to stay in Denver and put our faith in Kate's fake documents," Jules told him, her voice scratchy. "We're still not sure how he found my mom, but when he caught up with her, he put her in the hospital."

She felt Garrett's sudden intake of breath. "What happened?"

"He beat her up, sexually assaulted her and, after realizing she was more hurt than he thought, took her to the hospital. He told everyone she was in a car accident, and because he's charming and polished and educated and because he flashed his police creds, they believed him. He was told that she'd be in hospital for a week, so he returned to Boston, which was where we were from originally. He asked for some vacation time…"

"What work did he do for the police?"

"My father was a lieutenant in the Boston PD, highly decorated, highly respected. Highly connected."

Garrett's arms tightened, and he released a low curse. Lifting his arms, he crisscrossed them across her torso, holding her a little tighter. "Tell me all of it, Jules."

No, she couldn't. Not all of it. But she'd tell him enough. "He picked up his truck and drove back to Denver. It took him two days. Somewhere around Des Moines, he fell asleep, and his car veered into oncoming traffic. He had a head-on collision with a truck and was killed instantly."

He didn't say anything and for that she was grateful.

"I was here, riding with Peta, playing with the dogs, in my happy place, blissfully unaware of all the drama. A few weeks later, my mom came to get me, and they told me that my dad was dead. I couldn't mourn him, and I was…relieved, I guess. He couldn't hurt my mom anymore, and we were free."

"Totally understandable," Garrett murmured, his breath warm against her temple. "I'm so glad that you were here, with Kate, and that you didn't have to see your mom in the hospital."

She was, too. "I feel safe here, like nothing can touch me. If I feel upset or stressed, I come to the ranch, and I find myself again."

He tightened his hold, and Jules felt safe in his arms, like he was the steel barrier between her and the often-ugly world. Then Garrett kissed the top of her head before stepping back. "Our coffee is getting cold. And then I think I should head upstairs and take a look at Kate's paperwork."

Jules took the cup of coffee he held out and wrapped her hands around the warm mug. She blew across the steaming liquid and took a sip. It wasn't as good as the coffee at his place, but it warmed her up from the inside out. Or was that Garrett? Was having him stand next to her, albeit temporarily, making her feel optimistic, more centered and a lot more at peace?

It was most likely the ranch, she decided. Being

here, in the middle of nowhere, surrounded by the mountains, always made her feel less stressed and more settled. She cocked her head to the side, remembering how devastated Garrett had looked the night before.

"If you take some time, walk the land, breathe its air, this place has a way of seeping into your soul. I've always found the answers I need here."

"What makes you think I need answers, Juliana?" Garrett asked, his tone light. But he couldn't fool her. She knew he had problems to work through. There was far more to his conversation with James than a simple job offer.

"Everyone has questions and we all need answers, Garrett. Step outside, get out of your head and let the mountains talk to you," Jules suggested, walking toward the door that led into the great room. "There's magic in the air here, Garrett. And it can heal you if you let it."

Six

Over the years, Garrett had developed the ability to look at financial documents and analyze and identify anomalies while mentally working his way through other issues.

In Kate's book-filled study, he perused Crazy Kate's profit-and-loss statements and thought about Jules's past. Anyone looking at her social-media platforms would think that she was a free spirit, a hard-working but fun-loving minor celebrity. But there was so much more to her than the facade she presented to the world. She was born into a life filled with tension, uncertainty and violence. Thinking of a young Jules being scared made him wish he could go back in time, as he'd find great pleasure in rearranging her father's face. Violence against women and children was the hallmark of a petty, small-minded man who, in his opinion, had some pretty major psychological issues.

Kate should never have built a new bottling plant.

Garrett was grateful Jules had Kate to run to, that she'd found freedom and love and affection. He had never had a ranch or a place or a person to give him comfort, to guide his way. He'd had to figure it out on his own.

Mmm, it's obvious Kate expanded too fast and too aggressively...

Jules and Kate were close, but he'd never been able to talk to his mom, and when he tried, she shut him down. Hard. His efforts to corroborate that Callum was his father had never borne any fruit, and her inability to explain the circumstances around his birth left him confused. Was he not worth an explanation? Did he mean so little? Why was protecting Callum more important than knowing how he came into the world?

But, as it turned out, all his conclusions and assumptions were false, and he felt like a fool. James, not Callum, was his father, and for some reason James no longer wanted to keep his identity a secret.

Damn, Kate's interest charges are through the roof...

Why did James want to kick over the Ryder-White applecart?

By asking him to become Ryder International's new CEO, by explaining that he and Emma had had a hot love affair when he was in his early twenties that had resulted in a child, James was risking everything: his home, his position and his goddamn inheritance. Was James at war with Callum? Was Garrett being used as a weapon? A pawn? As a means to an end?

Garrett hadn't built up an empire by rushing blindly into situations, and he didn't intend to make any impulsive moves. Besides, he wasn't a kid anymore who craved a family; he was perfectly fine on his own.

Games were being played, and Garrett still needed to learn the rules. So, for now, he'd keep James at arm's length until he had a better handle on how this situation would play out.

Why the hell did Kate sign a new distribution agreement when things were so dire?

Garrett promised to give James an answer about the CEO position within the next week, and he regretted doing that. He needed a lot more time. Honestly, he should've refused on the spot, as he didn't have the time, or the energy, to run another multibillion dollar organization. He'd sweated blood and tears to establish Kaye Capital, and he was not going to put his business at risk for someone else's.

He also needed to speak to his mother, to get confirmation of James's wild claims.

Garrett raised his head and looked out the window, expecting to see a clear day. But heavy, dark clouds had rolled in, covering the amazing view of the Rocky Mountains. Peta had called it: those clouds looked ominous. Man, he was so sick of winter.

Garrett turned his attention back to Kate's computer, scanning the files for an asset register. He was hoping to find something massively undervalued, a cache of items that someone had overlooked.

The bottom line was that she'd experienced chronic cash-flow problems and had needed a loan to cover her expenses. Then she'd needed another loan when her cash flow didn't improve. Because she was over-extended and because she was emotionally attached to Crazy Kate's, she had remortgaged this property, thinking that it was a temporary bump, something she could easily recover from. She had been wrong.

Garrett looked at his watch, raising his eyebrows at the time. Thanks to the low-lying clouds blocking out the sun, two in the afternoon felt like dusk. He wondered how much more time he should give Kate's financials, as he knew, deep down in his gut, that she was bankrupt and would soon be homeless.

And Jules would lose her happy place.

He could go downstairs, tell her that Kate didn't have a chance of saving her ranch, and their weekend would end abruptly. Or he could delay. Would it make any difference if he told her tomorrow, before they left? It was the weekend, and thirty-six hours wouldn't make an iota of difference, and he'd get to spend some more time with the very intriguing Jules.

She fascinated him, as she was far more than a pretty face and a quick quip. Beneath the charming bartender was a woman with more layers than he could ever have imagined. Judging by their kiss, their sexual chemistry was off the charts, and he really wanted to see her naked.

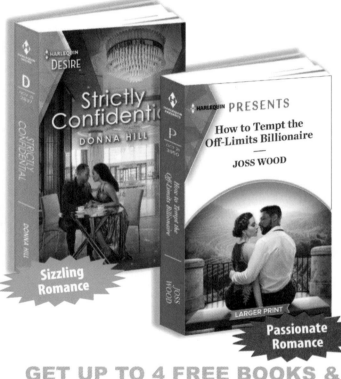

Get ready to relax and indulge with your **FREE BOOKS** and more!

Claim up to FOUR NEW BOOKS & TWO MYSTERY GIFTS – absolutely FREE!

Dear Reader,

We both know life can be difficult at times. That's why it's important to treat yourself so you can relax and recharge once in a while.

And I'd like to help you do this by sending you this amazing offer of up to FOUR brand new full length FREE BOOKS that WE pay for.

This is everything I have ready to send to you right now:

Try **Harlequin® Desire** books featuring the worlds of the American elite with juicy plot twists, delicious sensuality and intriguing scandal.

Try **Harlequin Presents® Larger-Print** books featuring the glamorous lives of royals and billionaires in a world of exotic locations, where passion knows no bounds.

Or **TRY BOTH!**

All we ask in return is that you answer 4 simple questions on the attached Treat Yourself survey. You'll get **Two Free Books** and **Two Mystery Gifts** from each series you try, *altogether worth over $20!* Who could pass up a deal like that?

Sincerely,

Pam Powers

Harlequin Reader Service

Treat Yourself to Free Books and Free Gifts.

Answer 4 fun questions and get rewarded.

◀ DETACH AND MAIL CARD TODAY! ▶

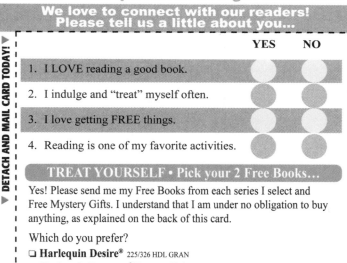

	YES	NO
1. I LOVE reading a good book.		
2. I indulge and "treat" myself often.		
3. I love getting FREE things.		
4. Reading is one of my favorite activities.		

TREAT YOURSELF • Pick your 2 Free Books...

Yes! Please send me my Free Books from each series I select and Free Mystery Gifts. I understand that I am under no obligation to buy anything, as explained on the back of this card.

Which do you prefer?

❏ **Harlequin Desire®** 225/326 HDL GRAN
❏ **Harlequin Presents® Larger-Print** 176/376 HDL GRAN
❏ **Try Both** 225/326 & 176/376 HDL GRAY

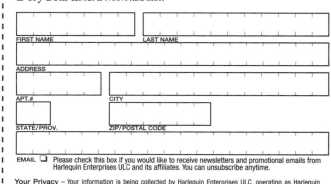

FIRST NAME   LAST NAME

ADDRESS

APT.#   CITY

STATE/PROV.   ZIP/POSTAL CODE

EMAIL ❏   Please check this box if you would like to receive newsletters and promotional emails from Harlequin Enterprises ULC and its affiliates. You can unsubscribe anytime.

HD/HP-520-TY22

BUSINESS REPLY MAIL
FIRST-CLASS MAIL   PERMIT NO. 717   BUFFALO, NY

POSTAGE WILL BE PAID BY ADDRESSEE

HARLEQUIN READER SERVICE
PO BOX 1341
BUFFALO NY 14240-8571

NO POSTAGE
NECESSARY
IF MAILED
IN THE
UNITED STATES

▼ If offer card is missing write to: Harlequin Reader Service, P.O. Box 1341, Buffalo, NY 14240-8531 or visit www.ReaderService.com ▼

But sex with Jules would be more than a way to get his rocks off. It wouldn't just be stress relief or something to do to pass the time. Making love with her would be more... Damn. More *what*?

He couldn't define it; he just knew it would be different. And after years of the same, he was in the mood for something a little out of the ordinary. Nothing permanent, but something to break up the sameness.

Work, exercise, sex. Work some more.

He was at a luxury ranch. He'd found out who his real father was. He'd been offered a new job. Wasn't that enough to shake him out of his complacency?

No, not nearly. He wanted Jules. But having her wasn't going to be easy. She was a curious mixture of street smarts and naivety, of confidence and fear. She was attracted to him, of that he was sure, but he had no idea whether she intended to act on their mutual attraction. And how far would she go to explore the passion bubbling between them?

She'd said she was a virgin, and her reasons for remaining so were a mystery. What was she waiting for? Love? Marriage?

She was looking in the wrong place if she expected either from him. He was the son of a woman who wore her single-mom status as a badge of honor—as she should. But he sometimes felt that Emma used him as a weapon to advance the idea of how capable she was, how much she didn't need anyone else. She'd taught him, from a young age, to be independent, and he wasn't ready to make space for another person in his life. He didn't think he'd ever be.

But Jules did intrigue him...

Garrett turned at the sound of footsteps on the stairs, and there she was, looking relaxed and five years younger in a pair of loose jeans and a moss-green slouchy sweater. Only thick socks covered her feet, and the side of her face bore the unmistakable imprint of a ridged cushion.

"Have you been sleeping while I toiled away up here?" he mock-demanded, surprised to hear the teasing note in his voice. He never teased anyone, didn't even know if he was doing it right.

"I was reading a book and drifted off," Jules admitted, walking into the room and approaching the wooden desk. "Sorry, that was rude of me. And I didn't give you lunch."

Garrett waved her apology away. "I never sleep during the day, and if I was hungry, I'm perfectly capable of finding something to eat."

Jules picked up a folder, read the label and put it down again. "Did you find anything?"

Yeah, he'd realized that things were worse than he'd thought. Instead of telling her the truth—he'd decided he wanted the rest of the weekend with her—he shrugged.

"Still looking at files," he replied. It wasn't a lie.

Jules rested her hip against the desk and wrinkled her nose. "Kate and Peta are running later than they thought they would be. It's already started snowing in town, and it's about to dump down here. The weather service has upgraded the report, suggesting the storm is intensifying. There are warnings about slick roads and dropping temperatures. Peta has a little phobia about driving on icy roads, so they are going to stay in town tonight. If the weather clears, they'll be back tomorrow."

Jules nodded to the window, and Garrett saw snowflakes drifting in on the wind. "I don't know if we can drive out tomorrow. We might be stuck here for a day or two."

He needed to be back in Portland, but he couldn't control the weather. Because he was a practical guy, he asked whether the house had a generator and an adequate supply of water, food and wood.

"Kate's been living here all her life, Garrett. She's ready for anything. So, yes, yes and yes."

Right, they wouldn't starve or freeze. It was a good start. "If we're going to be stuck indoors for a while, do you want to take a walk while we can?"

Jules, to his surprise, nodded. "Kate asked me to feed their horses. Apparently they couldn't bring themselves to sell their favorite animals."

Garrett pushed his chair back and stood up, stretched. He walked around the desk and held out his hand. Jules placed her hand in his and flashed him a heart-stopping grin. "I also need to collect eggs. C'mon, city boy. Let's see how you do with chickens."

After feeding the two remaining horses—Kate's pinto and Peta's Arabian—and replacing the straw in their stables, Jules efficiently collected eggs from the chicken coop and filled up the feed troughs.

Despite being away for so long, her movements were familiar and instinctive, and there was peace in seeing to the livestock, what little of it there was.

Jules was conscious of Garrett's eyes on her, watching her work. He'd offered to help, but there was sadly so little to do that it was quicker to do it herself than to hand out instructions. She glanced at him, his hands bunched into the pockets of his parka, the beanie covering his eyebrows. Although he was from Portland, he moved from heated car to heated office to heated home and wasn't used to spending any amount of time in the cold.

To be honest, neither was she. She'd lost feeling in her nose twenty minutes ago, and her fingers were cramping with cold. It had been a long, long time since she'd spent a winter in the Rockies.

Jules shut the door to the chicken coop and stamped her feet. "Let's head back. I could murder a hot chocolate."

"I could murder a whiskey," Garrett countered. Taking her hands, he lifted them to his mouth. He blew on her icy fingers before taking off his soft leather gloves and rubbing her hands between his. "Man, your hands are freezing, Ju."

He had no idea. Thinking that he looked and felt far too warm, she lifted her free hand and slid her fingers down his neck, digging under his scarf and the collar of his jacket. He yelped and danced away. He mock-frowned at her, but she caught his small smile, the amusement flashing in his thunderstorm eyes.

"Let me warm them up on your hot, hot skin," Jules said in a breathy, baby-doll voice, fluttering her eyelashes for added effect.

She expected him to bat her away, to tell her she didn't have a chance in hell of warming her ice-block hands on him, but he surprised her when he lifted his arms away from his body. "Go for it."

Jules bit her lip, off guard. "I was just messing with you, Garrett."

"Hey, when a gorgeous woman asks to put her hands on me, I always, always say yes," Garrett replied, his husky voice causing little fireworks to pop on her skin.

Jules saw the challenge on his face, in his eyes, and her inner bad girl told her not to be a sissy, to accept the dare. Lifting one eyebrow, Jules moved closer to him and pushed her hands under his jacket, then under his cashmere jersey. She found the soft cotton of his Henley and tugged it from his pants, burrowing her hands under it to find his skin.

She placed her palms on the ridges of his stomach. Yum. It was like putting her hands in front of a fire.

But better. A thousand times better.

Her thumb drifted through the hair of his happy trail, and she wondered what he'd look like naked. Utterly fantastic, she suspected.

She heard Garrett release a hiss and felt his stomach muscles contract, but he didn't pull back. Moving her cold hands to his hips and then to his back, she burrowed in closer, burying her cold nose in his soft, woolen scarf. He was heat and heart, and she could stand here forever.

Just like this.

Jules felt his thumb skimming her cheek. She tipped her head back and saw desire blazing in his eyes. He tapped her cheekbone with his thumb. "You are so incredibly beautiful, Jules."

She knew she was pretty and, with a lot of work, could sometimes hit stunning. But she knew she wasn't beautiful. "I'm not wearing a stitch of makeup, and I have a red nose and red cheeks," she told him.

"Naturally beautiful," Garrett whispered. He tipped his head to the side. "Can I kiss you, Juliana-Jaliyah?"

Hell, when he used her full name in that particular voice, he could strip her naked and take her up against a wall. "I'd like you to, Garrett." But they had to be sensible. "But we're in a stable, the storm is picking up and I think it's best we went back to the house."

Garrett frowned, then sighed. "Sexy and sensible."

Jules reluctantly removed her hands from his body and lifted her still-cold fingers up to her mouth and blew hot air onto her hands. Garrett handed her his gloves. "Use these."

Jules shook her head. "I'm fine. We'll be back at the house in five minutes."

"You've been hauling water and working with cold buckets, so put them on, Jules," Garrett told her.

He had that stubborn look on his face that she was coming to recognize. He wasn't going to budge until he got his way. The wind was now howling, and she didn't want to stay in this barn arguing with him. Glaring at him, Jules slid her hands into the too-big wool-lined gloves. Her fingers immediately started tingling with relief.

Satisfied, Garrett put his hand on her back to usher her toward the barn door. "Anything else you need to do in here?" he asked.

"No, I think we're good. The horses have blankets, the barn is insulated and they'll be fine," Jules replied.

Garrett stepped in front of her to push open the big barn door, leaving them just enough space to slip into the night. Snow slapped her face, and Jules put her back to the barrage, watching as Garrett closed and latched the door.

Jules instinctively turned to the left, holding her hand out for Garrett to take. They hustled, hand in hand, back to the house, trying to ignore the icy pellets in the wind and the wet sludgy snow hitting their faces and sliding down the backs of their collars.

Turning the corner, they saw the door to the kitchen and increased their pace, desperate to get back into the warmth and the light.

Garrett reached the door first, but instead of barreling inside, he yanked it open and waited for her to reach him. He shut the door behind them and, to her amusement, engaged the never-used dead bolt.

The nearest neighbor was ten miles away, and

they were in the ass-end of nowhere. Who did he think would pay them an unexpected visit?

He saw her laughing and sighed. "City boy, remember?"

Jules took off her beanie, unwound her scarf and dropped both on the small table in the mudroom. She hung her jacket on the hook by the door and stamped her feet to dislodge the stubborn snow before stepping out of her wet boots. Garrett followed her lead, and they walked into the kitchen in stocking feet.

Jules nodded to the door that separated the kitchen from the mudroom. "You're not going to lock that one, too?"

"Hey, there might be a psychotic Bigfoot wandering around out there."

"And you think a thin door is going to stop an eight-foot, big-as-hell man-ape?" Jules teased him.

Garrett started to reply, stopped and threw up his hands. "I've got nothing."

Jules laughed and walked over to the stove, where Kate's stew sat in a huge pot. She turned to face Garrett. "Are you hungry? We can have a late lunch, and if we get hungry later, I can warm up some soup. There's always soup in the freezer."

"Not right now," Garrett told her.

Jules turned to look at him, and all the moisture in her mouth disappeared as he stared at her, his expression intense. All his focus was on her, and she placed her hand on her heart as he walked around the table to reach her.

She expected him to place his hands on her and

yank her to him, to plunder her mouth and sweep them away on a tsunami of heat and hunger.

But Garrett stopped a foot from her and simply lifted his hand to swipe his thumb across her bottom lip. "You have such a sexy mouth, and I need to have it under mine again."

She couldn't speak, couldn't move, scared that this perfect, perfect moment would dissolve like a bubble hitting a spike of grass.

"I want to kiss you, Ju."

Words were impossible, so she simply nodded and waited for his mouth to reach hers, for their passion—so combustible—to ignite.

Initially, his kiss was soft, almost chaste. His lips nibbled hers, feeding her small, soft kisses. Jules released a growl of frustration, and she felt his lips curve against hers.

"More?" he whispered.

She draped an arm around his neck and stood up on her tiptoes. "More," she replied.

He laughed at her impatience and simply resumed his teasing. Frustrated, Jules palmed the back of his head, held his jaw in her other hand and pressed her mouth to his, sliding her tongue past his teeth.

Her tongue wove around his, and she felt him tense. He stepped into her space and, with one hand on her lower back, pulled her closer, so close that her stomach pushed into his hard, oh-so-lovely erection.

Better, Jules thought.

But it could be so much more. She pulled her

mouth off his and looked up at him. "Kiss me, Kaye. Properly."

"Your wish is my command, princess," Garrett replied.

Just to tease her, he waited another ten seconds, but when he resumed kissing her, he dialed the heat up to nuclear, and suddenly, Jules didn't know which way was up or down. His mouth ravaged hers—there was no other word for it—and she, in turn, wanted to inhale him. To climb inside him and hang out there...

Garrett's hands skated over her butt and snuck up and under her sweater, bare fingers dipping down the gap between her jeans and her lower back. She shivered as his long fingers ran up her spine, skirting her rib cage, inching closer to her breasts.

She wanted him to touch her there, to touch her *everywhere*.

Needing her hands on him, she pulled up his Henley and placed her cold hands on his skin. Her hands discovered the light covering of hair on his pecs, his flat nipples, the hard muscle under his masculine skin. Her fingers danced over his ladderlike stomach and flirted with the band of his pants, knowing that if she moved an inch, she'd be able to press her palm against his hard length.

She wanted to do that, she really did...

So she did.

God, this wasn't like her, allowing passion to take her on a dizzy ride. She never allowed things to move this fast, but then again, this was Garrett, and he was different.

"I want to look at you, see you naked. Is that okay?"

Jules nodded, and he pulled her sweater up and over her head, stepping back to look at her in her thin lacy bra, her nipples visible.

He ran a finger across one nipple, then the other. "So beautiful."

Without giving her time to react, he dropped down to kiss her, tugging her distended bud into his mouth. Jules whimpered, and before moving to the other breast, he pulled the lace away. Then his tongue was on her skin, and she arched her back, shoving her fingers into his hair to keep him there, doing that. Hopefully forever.

Garrett adored her breasts for a long time before sliding his mouth down her sternum, kissing her stomach, licking her navel. He sank to his knees, and Jules was so caught up in the way he made her feel that she didn't protest when he slid down the zipper to her jeans, placing kisses on the triangle of her lacy panties. Her jeans slid over her hips, and at his order, Jules lifted her foot and stepped out of one leg.

"Widen your legs, sweetheart."

Oh, no, he couldn't be doing this, not in Kate's kitchen. Embarrassed, Jules was about to call a halt to the proceedings, but Garrett placed an open-mouthed kiss on her inner thigh, gently nipped her skin and soothed it with his tongue. He nuzzled her mound, making approving sounds and, with one gentle finger, pulled her panties aside. He blew warm air onto her, and Jules gripped the counter with both hands, wondering how much longer her legs would hold out.

Garrett rubbed his knuckle over her feminine lips, finding her bundle of nerves with unerring accuracy.

As his fingers and lips worked in unison to toss her toward the stars, Jules allowed her mind to soar and her spirit to dance with the night sky. Was that a comet to her right, a shooting star to her left? As her pleasure inched higher and higher, she saw black holes and supernovas, space dust and fairy lights.

And then, when Garrett slid two large fingers inside her and placed his skilled tongue on her clitoris, she stepped into the sun and detonated.

She didn't know if she screamed or cried or laughed—probably all three simultaneously—but her legs did buckle, and her knees liquefied. Garrett's arm encircled the top of her thighs, and he took her weight, tonguing her until she hit another, even bigger orgasm. Then her legs failed, and she dropped down, her thighs resting on his, her forehead on his shoulder.

"GodohGodohGod…"

Garrett's hand smoothed her hair. "That good, huh?"

"Geh…geh…gump…" Lord, she'd lost the ability to talk.

Garrett's laugh was low and completely wicked. "I'll take that as a yes." Wrapping his arms around her, he stood up, lifting his body weight and hers in one easy movement. He sat her on the kitchen counter and stepped between her legs. Holding her face in his hands, he dropped an openmouthed kiss on her mouth. She tasted herself—a little sweet, a lot sexy—on his tongue. God, that was hot.

"Take me upstairs, Juliana-Jaliyah," he murmured between kisses. "Take me up to your room, and let me make love to you, in a bed, as the snow falls outside."

Jules tensed and pulled back, ice invading her veins. Oh, God, she wanted to. She wanted him to carry her to her room and lay her down on her bed.

Up there she'd be able to see his strong, amazing body, experience what making love to a man was really about. In the silence, she'd hear his deep breathing, his voice on her skin.

She tried to hold on to that image but slamming doors, her father's drunken insults and her mother's cries, accompanied by the unmistakable sound of the bed slamming against a thin wall, rolled over her.

She heard his grunts, her sobs, and every muscle in her body tensed. Words like *slut* and *you'll take it and you'll damn well like it* echoed in her head, and she lifted her bunched fist to her mouth and cursed her shaking body.

"Jesus, Jules."

Strong arms picked her up off the counter, and Garrett walked her over to the rocking chair in the corner and sat down with her in his arms. He pulled the blanket lying on its back across her. Jules remembered that she was wearing nothing more than her panties and bra, both of which were askew. Under the blanket, Garrett pulled her bra cup across her breast, and she slid her hand between her legs to re-arrange her panties.

Jules buried her face in his neck and tried to stop

shaking. She'd been in this position before with other guys, she thought, but the memories had never been this vivid, her reaction so strong.

Why was she falling apart with Garrett?

And, God, he had to think her the biggest tease in the history of the world. Jules sniffed and wiped the ball of her hand across her burning eyes. "I'm so sorry. I shouldn't have let you go so far."

"Shh," Garrett murmured, his hand running up and down her bare thigh.

"I'm sorry."

"Nothing to be sorry for."

"But you didn't—"

"Not coming won't kill me, Jules." Garrett forced her head back onto his shoulder and gently held her. Jules breathed deeply—in for four, hold for four, out for four—and felt the memories recede, her tension fade away. She felt warm and relaxed, and if she closed her eyes, she could sleep.

"I suppose you want an explanation," she murmured, on a huge yawn.

"Only if you want to give me one."

She didn't, not now, possibly never. "Please don't be mad at me, Garrett."

She'd had anger from guys before. A few who told her she'd led them on, that she was a prick-tease and that she should be grateful for what she'd been offered.

"I'm not mad, sweetheart. Consent is me asking whether you want to be intimate with me. But it's also respecting your right to say no, at any point in the process."

This guy...

"I chose to love you like that. I enjoyed every second of it. But there's no expectation of quid pro quo."

She couldn't tell him everything, but maybe she could shed a little light on her messed-up mind. "It's not that I don't *want* to. I would've, if we'd stayed right there. Hell, if you'd hauled a condom out of your pocket, we might've even christened the table where Kate and Peta eat breakfast. I want you. Don't doubt that."

She felt his chest swell, as if he was holding his breath. "So correct me if I am wrong. You're not averse to sex per se, just sex in a bedroom?"

God, he was sharp. She'd tried to explain before, using the same words, but nobody understood. Or made the effort to understand.

"Well...*huh*."

Jules dropped her head back to look at his profile. "Is that all you have to say?"

He turned his head, smiled at her and dropped a kiss on her nose. "For now. Snuggle down and close your eyes... Feeding those horses exhausted me."

She smiled. "You just watched me. I did all the work." Jules felt his kiss in her hair as the chair started to rock. "If you keep rocking the chair, I'm going to fall asleep," she told him.

"Good, do that."

Feeling warm and relaxed and oh-so-lazy, Jules obeyed.

Seven

"How did Kate come to start up a gin-making business?" Garrett asked as Jules put a plate of steaming stew in front of him. The enormous wooden dining table stood in front of a massive window, and beyond the insulated panes, heavy snowflakes danced on the wind.

He'd never known darkness like this: it was complete, stygian, horror-movie black.

He rather liked it.

Garrett watched as Jules, after putting a plate of homemade bread between them, took her place next to him so that she could also, he presumed, look out onto the night.

She'd slept for about an hour, and strangely, he'd been happy to hold her, enjoying the quietness, letting his thoughts roll in and out, not feeling the need to solve any problems or plot strategy. He might even have dozed off, but if anyone asked, he'd deny that with his dying breath. He never napped. It wasn't what a constantly-on-the-go workaholic did.

Hell, Jules had a way of making him step out of the normal and embrace the...unexpected.

He didn't accompany acquaintances to ranches high in the Rockies to try and save a stranger's family farm. He didn't muck about in stables in the bitter cold. He didn't hold a woman while she slept.

Jules had the strangest effect on him.

"Before she met and married Peta, Kate was in a long-term relationship. He hated ranch life, she loathed the city and they quickly realized they were better off living apart. Seth bought a house in Denver, and Kate spent nights and weekends with him there," Jules explained, leaning back in her seat. The wide neck of her sweater exposed her shoulder and the strap of that lacy bra. He recognized that brand of lingerie. Their items were gloriously feminine, custom-made and brutally expensive.

Vouchers to order off the brand's online shop made excellent thanks-for-the-fling-we're-over gifts.

Garrett pulled his attention back to his earlier question and told himself to concentrate.

"They did marry at some point, shortly before I met her, I think. Seth owned a company making craft gin, and built up a small name for himself online and at gourmet-food markets. He named the company after Kate. He called her his crazy, wild child."

"So she wasn't always gay?"

Jules shrugged. "Kate told me that she's always been sexually fluid, more attracted to the mind than the body. Seth was an artist, a hippy, and from all accounts, he made her happy," Jules explained, after taking a couple bites of stew. "I never knew Seth but I think I would have liked him."

He followed her lead and sighed at the explosion of flavors on his tongue. "God, this is good."

"Kate can cook," Jules agreed. "Anyway, I was in my late teens when Seth was diagnosed with stage four pancreatic cancer. He died six weeks later."

Garrett stared at her, aghast. "That's quick."

"So quick. She was heartbroken."

"So to honor him, she took over his craft-gin company," Garrett said.

Jules took a bite of bread and waved her hand from left to right. "Sort of. She became a recluse for six months, maybe more. Then she started to work at the women's shelter in the city, and I met her maybe nine months after Seth died.

"She let the company languish, and it faded away. A couple of years later, Kate got a call from someone asking if he could buy Seth's gin recipes, his equipment, the Crazy Kate's name and his branding. Kate nearly sold it to him."

"What stopped her?" Garrett asked, interested.

"She'd met Peta by then at a grief-counseling group—Peta had lost her partner of twenty years in a car accident—and Peta suggested that before she sold anything to anybody, she should understand what she was selling and why. So Kate started working the business and soon found herself loving it. She made gin following Seth's recipes and then added flourishes of her own. She redesigned his website and reached out to his previous suppliers, and they were all ecstatic to carry her product. Soon, she couldn't keep up with demand."

Garrett could guess the rest. She bought a building and set up a commercial gin-making process. The orders, bigger and better, started rolling in, and to fulfill them, she borrowed more and more, thinking she'd repay the loans out of profits. But one client went into liquidation, another ran into cash-flow problems themselves, and she found herself in trouble. It was a book he'd read so many times. One he could've written himself.

"You said Kate gave you your start as a mixologist. How?" Garrett asked, wanting to move the subject off Kate and onto Jules.

She smiled. "She hired me to promote Crazy Kate's at state fairs and music festivals. I learned to make all the gin classics, but then I started experimenting with making other cocktails, some of which were horrible, some okay. I always seemed to have a crowd at my stand—" he could understand why as she was both gorgeous and charming "—and other drinks companies started hiring me to promote their products. When I finished college, I went to bartending school." Pointing her fork at him, she said, "And yes, there is such a thing. The jobs kept rolling in, and I was never short of work, and I loved traveling from town to town. I still do.

"During one of my trips back east, I auditioned to run a pop-up bar for Ryder International, and I met Tinsley and Kinga."

"You mentioned that, at the ball."

She wrinkled her nose in apology. "The three of us clicked straight away, and they hired me to fly to Hong Kong and do a demonstration in their newest Ryder Bar. I pretty much haven't stopped moving since."

"Don't you get sick of living in hotel rooms and eating restaurant food?" Garrett asked. He was on the road a lot, and after a couple of days, all he wanted was his own bed and fridge.

Jules ate a little stew before answering him. "Moving around was what I did for many, many years with my mom," she quietly explained. "Moving makes me feel secure. Staying in one place makes me antsy."

"Because of your dad," Garrett stated.

"Yeah, because of him." Jules stared down at her plate, idly pushing her food around. "Can we not talk about him or me?"

He didn't like people pushing him to open up, so he respected her wish to move on from her past and her parents. "One last question?" he said, as a thought popped into his head.

She lifted her eyebrows.

"Where does your mom live? You don't talk about her. You talk about Kate all the time, but your mom? Not so much."

Jules wrinkled her nose and placed her elbows on the table. "My mom still lives in Denver. She works as an aid in a retirement home. We don't talk much." She dredged up a smile. "I know you are going to ask me why not, and I'll tell you, but then we're done talking about me, okay?"

Garrett nodded.

"After my father died, life was good. Really good. We were so happy for a few years. In my final year of school, luckily just a few months before I graduated, she met a guy and fell for him. He moved in and within weeks was physically abusing her. She stayed with him and they are still together."

Garrett stared at her, astounded. "No way."

"After *everything* my father did and what she went through, it's hard to believe, right?"

Garrett stared at her, unable to believe what he was hearing. "I'm sorry, I don't understand why she would do that."

Jules's shoulders hit her ears before dropping again. "I asked her the same question. She told me that it's not an issue and that he's nothing like my father. That she loves him and can't live without him." Jules rubbed the back of her neck. "I told her I couldn't watch it happen again and that she had to choose him or me. She chose him."

"Aw, baby."

"I don't like it, but I've learned to accept that it's her life and her choice to make."

Yeah, behind the gloss and the glamour was a

woman who'd been hurt a hundred times over. Garrett wished he could go back in time and kick some ass.

Jules wiped up some gravy with a piece of bread and popped it into her mouth. She gestured to the window and the darkness beyond it. "God, it's so beautiful and so quiet."

Garrett pushed his plate away and reached for his tumbler of whiskey. It was great whiskey, one of his favorites. He took a sip and felt the burn slide down his throat.

"Do you not drink anything other than whiskey?" Jules asked. When he shook his head, she looked horrified. "No wine, no beer?"

"Wine gives me a horrendous hangover, and beer doesn't float my boat. Cocktails are normally too sweet or taste like chemicals."

"Sacrilege!" Jules sent him a horrified look and placed her hand on her heart. "I have to change your mind. I have some kick-ass combinations for other spirits that you'll love."

He didn't think so, but he'd play this game as long as it made her smile. He placed his elbows on the table and smiled at her. "You can try, but my mind is not easily changed." He gestured to the drinks stand where he'd found the bottle of whiskey. "But do your best."

Jules sent it a sour look. "I'll have to take a rain check on that because Kate, despite being a crafter of one of the best gins I've ever tasted, doesn't keep much liquor in the house, and Peta doesn't drink at all." She smiled. "When we get back to Portland,

I'll invite you to Ryder Bar downtown and show you what I can do."

He'd suffer through a couple of revolting cocktails if it meant spending more time with her. Garrett ran his hand through his hair, thinking that he was a fly trapped in a particularly sticky web. And that he wasn't fighting too hard to extricate himself.

"What's your favorite cocktail?" Garrett asked, leaning back in his chair.

"I make an amazing version of a Moscow mule."

He pulled a face. "What's that, again?"

Jules grinned at him. "Vodka, ginger beer, lime juice. My version uses vegetable juices, carrot mostly, lots of fresh ginger and cilantro."

It sounded awful, and he told her so. "That's a salad, not a drink," he grumbled.

"Don't knock it until you try it, Kaye." Jules pointed her finger at him. "And you will try it."

He laughed at her fierceness, amused that she thought she could get him to do something he didn't want to do. That hadn't happened in a long, long time. But deep inside, Garrett suspected this woman might be the person he'd make an exception for. She'd gotten him to fly to Colorado ahead of a record-breaking snow dump. Hell, who knew what he'd be agreeing to next?

Feeling uncomfortable with the direction of his thoughts, Garrett pulled his eyes off her lovely face and looked outside. "Hey, it's stopped snowing, and the wind has died down."

"Not for long," Jules muttered. "I checked the weather report, and it's supposed to snow all night."

"But it's not snowing now."

Jules looked outside and shrugged. "So?"

"Let's take a walk," Garrett suggested. It was either walk or kiss her senseless, and he didn't know if he'd cope with another bout of lovemaking that was interrupted halfway through. No, it was better to find something else to do, some other way to distract them.

"In subzero temperatures?"

It was a reasonable alternative to a cold shower.

Jules, looking like the Abominable Snowman, plodded along next to Garrett, her rain boots sinking into the snow. The clouds had parted, just for a moment, to show a star-studded sky and a full moon. It wouldn't last, but she was happy to stand next to Garrett and imagine plucking the moon from the sky, as if it were a bright, silver apple.

Jules thought that she would be quite content to stand with Garrett anywhere.

He was blunt and terse but so honest, and the way he looked at her heated her blood.

She wasn't an idiot: she knew he wanted her with a ferocity that shocked her. That she could turn him on—this man who dated movie stars and models—was a hell of an ego boost. And his willingness to stop—to hold her when she freaked out, to not complain or demand an explanation—warmed her.

Jules felt like she could tell him anything, that he

was pretty much unshockable. Could she tell him about her father, how his actions led to her fear of sex…?

No! She had to stop thinking that.

She didn't fear *sex*. She would've happily allowed Garrett to finish what they'd started if he hadn't mentioned them moving to the bedroom. Hell, he could've taken her on the kitchen floor or on Kate's sturdy dining table. No, the act itself didn't frighten her, but she didn't want her first time to be tainted with the memory of her father gripping her mom's hair, pulling her to their bedroom at the end of the hall.

Why had she never realized this before? Why had it taken her so long to work this out? And why hadn't she asked any of those other guys to do her on the couch or the dining table or the rug in her living room?

She was pretty sure they wouldn't have minded. She enjoyed kissing, touching, the feel of a man's body plastered against hers and the different textures, smells and sounds they had.

So why had she hesitated?

Jules forced herself to dig deep, to get to the heart of the matter. Surely, if she was so affected by how her father treated her mother after a fight, she'd be terrified of the sex act, not just scared of being alone in a bedroom with a man? What was the difference with being alone with a man in her living room? She was still behind a closed door.

Jules thought about her previous relationships,

remembering the few hot-and-heavy encounters of her past. They'd get down and dirty, indulge in some heavy petting and maybe some oral sex, but when the man of the moment asked to move to the bedroom, she shut down…just like she had with Garrett earlier.

He'd phone the next day, and the day after, send emails and text messages, and eventually she'd reply, quickly finding an excuse not to see him again.

Months would pass, she'd meet someone else, and the whole dysfunctional cycle would repeat itself.

At this rate, she'd be an eighty-year-old virgin.

Had she been using her fear of sex to avoid starting something with somebody? Was she scared that opening the door to her sexuality would open the door to love, to commitment, a future? It didn't have to be like that. Having sex didn't mean that she had to commit to a guy. Sex was sex; love was different.

Garrett didn't want a relationship. That wasn't something he expected from her. If she slept with him, nothing would change between them. And wasn't it time to get past this, to put her issues behind her?

She was almost thirty years old and was a modern woman in thought and deed. She deserved an active, fun sex life. And if anyone could help her move past this, Garrett—the first person who fried her brain and caused a massive lowering of her inhibitions—could.

"Would you sleep with me?" she demanded, her voice loud in the silent night.

And just like that, a cloud covered the moon. Jules

imagined it slapping its hand over its eyes, mortified at her blunt, out-of-the-blue question.

Garrett turned to face her, his expression inscrutable. "That came out of nowhere."

"Tell me about it," Jules grumbled, kicking a clump of snow with the toe of her boot.

"What's changed since earlier?" Garrett asked her, using a bland, nothing-to-see-here voice.

"I'd like to…" God, this was embarrassing "…complete the act. I'd like to stop feeling like a jittery spinster and have a life that includes sex. And I'd like you to help me with that."

Garrett ran his hand over his face. "Maybe you should think about this, Jules. Choose someone who's a little kinder, someone with more patience."

Jules stomped her foot. "I tried that, and it didn't work." She looked away, conscious of the heat warming her face from the inside out. "Look, nobody has ever made me feel the way you do."

She saw horror drop into his eyes and saw him pull back, as if he were stepping away from her words. She waved her hands around. "I'm not asking you to marry me, Kaye! I'm just trying to tell you that I've never felt so physically attracted to anybody as I do to you."

"Okay…right. Good."

Jeez, he didn't have to look so relieved.

Garrett rocked on his heels, his face an unreadable mask. "I'm not sure if this is a good idea, Jules."

"For you or me?" Jules challenged him.

They stepped onto Kate's wraparound deck, and

thanks to the outdoor lighting, Jules could see the hesitation on his face. "Look, if you don't want to, then just say so, and I'll move on."

"To what? To whom?" Garrett demanded.

"I don't know, but I can't keep living like this! I can't keep bailing, running from the memory!"

Garrett's eyes sharpened. "What memory?"

"He'd beat her and then drag her into the bedroom. She'd cry, plead, but…crap, the walls were thin." Jules rubbed the back of her neck, feeling uncomfortable. "As I said, I have a thing about bedrooms."

Garrett stared at her for the longest time, his expression inscrutable. Was he regretting being here with her? Thinking that this was too much information, that she was being too dramatic? Damn, she shouldn't have let that slip. It was her biggest secret, something she'd never shared before. She gestured to the door leading into the great room. "I'm going in."

Garrett looked up at the sky where clouds were rolling back in. "Yep, here comes round two."

Jules walked down the side of the house until she came to the door to the mudroom and yanked it open. They shed outer layers and shoes and, in silence, walked into the large house, the silence broken by the crackle of logs in the overlarge fireplace.

Jules put her hands out to the flames, sighing when she heard Garrett running up the stairs. A door opened and closed, and she wondered where he'd gone and whether he was coming back.

Who'd have thought that asking for sex would be so hard?

Jules stared into the gold-and-blue flames, remembering how many times she'd fallen asleep on that leather couch, staring at the fire. How secure and safe she felt with Kate upstairs and the dogs gently snoring in their dog beds scattered throughout the room.

This was her happy place, her refuge, her safe place.

God, what was she going to do if it passed out of Kate's hands? Jules sighed, embarrassed at her selfishness. She made it out here a few times a year, but this was where Kate and Peta lived. They had an emotional connection to this ranch that was far stronger than hers. She'd be so sad to lose Kilconnell Ranch, but Kate would be devastated.

There had to be something someone could do. But Garrett had looked at the books earlier and hadn't found anything. What if there was nothing to find? What then?

Jules felt Garrett's arms encircle her waist, sighed when his lips touched the spot where her shoulder met her neck. He was so much taller than her, so much stronger, yet she felt safe with him, protected. Was that why she'd asked him to sleep with her?

Why did she instinctively know that he'd never hurt her? Was she confusing lust with trust, thinking that, because he'd set off a series of explosions in her womb, between her legs, he was trustworthy?

No, she wasn't that easily confused.

"Do you want to explain some more? Talk about it?" he asked, his question gentle.

"No, I want you to love me."

Garrett lifted the hair off her neck, pushed it over her shoulder and, using his tongue, painted streaks of fire over her skin, along the cords of her neck. Gently turning her around, he placed his mouth on hers, his tongue between her lips, asking her to let him in. Jules placed her hands on his pecs and stood on her tiptoes, eager to explore his mouth, to have him in hers.

His hand skimmed down her throat, across her shoulder and down her torso, his fingertips coming to rest on her puckered nipple. She arched her back, wanting to get closer to him, needing more.

"Let's get your clothes off, baby," Garrett whispered.

Jules tipped her head back and looked up into his serious face. "So are we doing this?"

"We'll go as far as you want. And if you want to call it quits, we stop. You're in control here, Ju."

Jules swallowed as he gently pulled her sweater up her body and over her head. The appreciation in Garrett's eyes made her feel supermodel gorgeous. He ran a finger down the slope of her shoulder, down her arm. "You have the most beautiful skin."

Jules tugged at his sweater, and Garrett reached behind him and, with one hand, pulled his sweater and T-shirt over his head and dropped them to the floor. Jules immediately placed her hands on his chest and her mouth above his heart, inhaling his sexy, turned-on, shower-and-soap smell. Gorgeous.

With a twist of his hand, Garrett undid her bra and pulled it down her arms, dropping the lacy fabric to the floor. One hand covered her breast, and he played with her nipple, his long fingers sending ribbons of pleasure dancing through her. Garrett bent his knees, wrapped his arms around the back of her thighs and easily lifted her so that her torso was aligned with his mouth. He pulled her nipple, flattening the bud against the roof of his mouth.

So strong, so powerful.

After telling her to wind her legs around his hips, he walked backward and lowered them both to the leather couch, with Jules sitting astride him, his hard shaft between her legs. There was too much fabric between them, and she wanted it gone.

Jules lifted her hands to hold his face and stared into those blue-green eyes. "I'm loving this, but…"

"But?" Garrett asked when she hesitated.

"We do it here, we don't move," Jules said.

Garrett nodded, his gaze solemn. "Deal." He kissed her again, starting slow and letting their passion build, his hands exploring her torso and back, occasionally swiping her nipples with his thumb before darting off to discover her ribs, her lower back, the soft skin above her jeans-covered hips.

Garrett pulled away from her mouth and ducked his head to kiss her breast, curling his tongue around her nipple. Jules closed her eyes, thinking that this was the best sexual encounter of her life.

"I need to see you naked, baby," Garrett suggested. He easily lifted her off his lap and tugged her between his legs, flicking open the button to her jeans and pulling down her zipper. He placed kisses on each inch of bare skin he exposed, and by the time her jeans skimmed down her hips, Jules was shaking with need.

She felt the throbbing between her legs, the warmth and the wet, and when Garrett pushed her panties down, she stiffened.

"Shh, Jules," Garrett murmured, dragging his finger down her narrow strip of hair. He slid his fingers between her feminine folds and into her wet channel, skimming her happy spot.

"So, so lovely," Garrett muttered. "The things I'd love to do to you, Juliana-Jaliyah."

Right now, she just wanted him inside her, stretching her. Rocketing her to an intense orgasm.

"You've got too many clothes on," Jules told him, shocked by the need in her voice. Reaching down, she aimed for the button on his jeans, but Garrett pushed her hands away, flipping open the top button, then the next. He slid his hands under his underwear—plain black and expensive—and lifted his hips, pushing his jeans and briefs down his hips. Jules couldn't take her eyes off his shaft, as big and long as he was, jutting out from a thick thatch of hair. She swallowed, wondering how she could accommodate him...

Garrett sent her a smile. "It'll be fine, Jules. Trust me."

She nodded, saw the reassurance in his eyes and nodded again.

Garrett lightly stroked her right thigh. His touch
was both reassuring and sexy, a curious combination of heat and encouragement. His hands skated
down her legs in a tactile assault that liquefied her
knees. She rested her hands on his shoulders and
stared down at his wavy hair, wishing he'd return
to that place between her legs where she ached the
most. Garrett looked up at her, and she swallowed
when she noticed the passion in his now-dark eyes,
his needy expression.

"Kiss me, Ju," he commanded, and Jules hooked
her thighs over his and slid down his legs, her mouth
connecting with his as her hot core slammed against
his shaft.

So, so good.

Their lips locked, tongues intertwined, and his fingers traced patterns on the bare skin of her butt. Her
panties created friction between them that they both
liked, the lace scratchy against her core. Garrett's hand
moved up and down her side, from ribs to breastbone,
occasionally spreading his fingers so that he brushed
her nipples. She felt enveloped by him, surrounded,
and she loved it. Her breasts pushed against his strong
chest, her hard nipples pressing into his skin. Needing
to touch him, to stoke his fire, she stroked his ribs,
tracing her fingers over his washboard stomach. He
felt amazing, and he made her feel desired, hot, horny.

Jules pushed her hands behind her, running them
over the parts of his thighs she could reach, rocking her core against his erection and feeling her heat
build. His hands cupped her breasts, teasing her nip-

ples. He ducked his head, kissed her jaw, sucked on her earlobe and told her that he wanted her mouth again. Sitting up, she leaned forward and slapped her mouth against his, their kisses turning feverish. She wanted to get closer, climb inside him, have him be inside her.

She'd never wanted anything more.

Unable to wait, she wrenched her mouth off his and pulled back to meet his eyes. She needed his complete attention, needed him to know that he was what she wanted, in every way that mattered. "I want you... Now," she added, her tone fierce.

"Not yet," Garrett muttered, lifting her off him. He lowered her to the Persian rug on the floor, and Jules looked up at him, her body pulsing with need.

"Garrett, please," Jules begged, trying to wrap her hand around his biceps to tug him down. But Garrett simply shook his head and moved his hands to her panties and, with one quick twist, snapped the thin cord at her hips. He slowly pulled the fabric out, dragging the lace across her clit, causing Jules to arch her back.

"More...of that!" she gasped.

"As you please, princess," Garrett said, amused. He slid his hands between her legs, brushed her clit and slid two fingers deep inside her. He did something, hit something, and Jules felt herself rocket up, releasing a series of low moans. He kept moving his fingers inside her and, with his other hand, rolled her nipple between his fingers. Jules closed her eyes in exquisite pleasure. He sat back on his knees and reached for his jeans, pulling condoms from the back pocket before tossing the pants to the side. He tore a condom off the strip, removed the latex from the packet and pushed it into Jules's hand.

God, they were really doing this.

"Put it on me, Jules. Touch me."

At his words, Jules realized that she'd been the one receiving pleasure and had handed out little herself. Sitting up, she wrapped her hand around his erection, exploring his silk, satin and steel member. She looked down and realized that even this part of him was beautiful.

At some point, not now, she wanted to kiss him, to take him into her mouth...

"Condom, Jules," Garrett reminded her.

At his gruff suggestion, her eyes flew to his face, and she saw the impatience in his eyes, the need on his face. Smiling, pleased that she could make such a powerful man shake with desire, she slowly, oh-so-slowly, rolled the condom down him, letting her fingers drift lower.

Garrett sucked in a harsh breath, and he put a hand on her shoulder and pushed her down. Reaching up, he snagged a cushion from the couch and told her to lift her hips, then he shoved the cushion under her bum.

He tested her readiness again—she was even wetter than before—and he positioned himself above her, his palms flat on the carpet next to her head, his penis sliding over her clitoris.

"Are you sure you want this, Jules?"

She nodded.

"Not good enough. Tell me," Garrett insisted as his tip rested against her bundle of nerves.

"I want you, Garrett. I need you," Jules said, almost weeping with frustration.

He slid inside her with one smooth stroke, pushed through the thin barrier and seated himself deeply.

He pulled back, and she protested. Garrett pushed her hair off her forehead, before sliding into her again. He started to repeat the action, cursed and tensed, choosing to move into her with care.

She didn't need that: she wanted him wild and unrestrained. "Take me, Garrett."

Garrett rested his weight on one elbow to push a strand of hair off her cheek. "We need to go slow, take it easy."

"I don't want easy or slow, I want hot and wild."

"Baby, you've never done this before..."

"With you, I feel like I have, like this is familiar," Jules insisted. She stroked his jaw with her fingertips. "Take me, Garrett. Hard."

He searched her face again, frowned and then sighed. His hand moved between their bodies and he slipped his finger down, finding her bud, which he stroked. Once, then twice, his hips lifting when Jules lifted her hips to slam herself against him. Heat and power and electricity and pleasure rolled through her, and she pulled Garrett's hand away.

Garrett heard her silent pleas and slammed into her. Jules sucked in a deep breath, thinking that he felt bigger than he had moments before. He rocked back, withdrawing to his limit before pounding into her again, and Jules, for the first time in her life, saw stars.

On the next thrust, those stars exploded, and on the next, her world disintegrated in tiny pinpricks of luminescent fragments.

From a space a million miles away, she felt Garrett's release, heard his shout, but she was spinning away on a tornado of color and sensation.

Eight

Jules, shattered and shaken, pulled the multipattern blanket off the back of the couch and wrapped it around her. She looked over to the window to where Garrett stood, magnificent in his nakedness. His forearm rested on the glass above his head and she wondered what he was thinking about as he looked out into the night.

She didn't regret making love to him. It had been a wonderful experience that she'd always remember. But while she might've lost her virginity, she was only halfway to resolving her bedroom problem. She'd never feel comfortable in an old-fashioned marriage, one where the man was the dominant partner, where his career took precedence over hers, where he got the final say on all decisions made.

She was scared of strong men, domineering men, men who were like her father. But more than that, she was scared that she would turn out to be like her mother, sacrificing herself to love and be loved.

Frightened that the deeper she immersed herself in the relationship, the less empowered she would be. Jules knew she was a lot like her mother, in both looks and personality, and she was terrified that if she fell in love, she'd lose herself.

Just like her mom had.

So don't fall in love.

Jules stared at Garrett's broad back, the way his spine dented in a masculine sweep just above his buttocks, his long, muscled legs. She'd never give a man the power over her, but she wouldn't mind having someone in her life, someone to come home to, a manly someone who would be glad to see her after days or weeks away. A man to wake up with, whose shoulder she could fall asleep on.

But that meant breaking through the final barrier and taking Garrett up to her bedroom and making love to him in her bed. In any bed. Maybe if she got past this hurdle, she could also sleep in a bed by herself, like everyone else.

Her breath hitched, and a vision of her father's big hand wrapped around her mother's hair, her neck bent at an impossible angle, flashed through her mind. She remembered a slick of drool in the corner of his mouth and a dangerous cocktail of power and passion in his hard, dark eyes.

Even as young as she was, Jules had known that bad things happened behind closed bedroom doors.

But her father had had a hold on her for too long, and she was still letting his actions affect her life. It had to stop.

She'd given Garrett her body, and he'd treated her well, very well indeed. And intellectually, she knew that nothing would change if she walked up the second flight of stairs to her attic bedroom. But her heart still wanted to beat out of her chest, and her mouth felt like she was trying hard not to swallow spiders.

But she had to do this. She had to cross this bridge. Garrett was here, and she didn't think he'd turn down an offer of round two.

Be brave, Jules.

"Will you come upstairs with me?"

She saw his spine straighten, the tension in his shoulders. He stepped back from the glass, and she saw that he was looking at her reflection in the window, just as she was looking at his. "I presume you are not asking me to come up to your room to play tiddlywinks?"

She hauled a deep breath into her collapsed lungs. "No, I'd like you to make love to me again, in my bedroom."

"Are you using me to banish some ghosts, Juliana?"

It killed her when he said her name in that way, all deep and dangerous. Jules thought about lying to him but lifted her shoulders in a quick shrug. She gestured to the carpet. "That was an amazing experience, and I'd like to do it again. This time I'd like to change the venue."

"Are you going to ravish me again, Juliana? Twice in one evening?"

She rolled her eyes at the hand he placed on his heart, his look of mock outrage. A small smile tipped the corners of his mouth up and the anticipation in his eyes told her he was up for, and looking forward to, round two.

"I'm sure you can handle me." She had no doubt about that.

Jokes aside, Garrett could and would handle whatever life threw his way. Because he was unemotional and practical, he stood his ground as emotion rolled over him, not allowing his feelings to move his eyes off the goal.

She needed someone like him to help her over this final hurdle, someone steady and sure. Someone she could lean on.

Someone she trusted.

Why did she trust him? She barely knew the man, but he had a mile-wide streak of integrity running through him. Yeah, his rep in the business world wasn't teddy bears and roses, but the world saw what they wanted to see. Hell, her followers assumed she was a super confident, kick-ass mixologist who frequently spoke out against domestic- and child-abuse issues, sexual harassment and humanitarian crises. Nobody, not even her best friends, knew she was scared of bedrooms…and what happened between those four walls.

It was time to get over it.

Garrett slowly turned and glided toward her, stopping a few feet from her. "Are you sure that's what you want to do?"

No. But Jules nodded.

"I don't want to kill the mood but I'm not your therapist," Garrett growled, but the worry in his eyes negated his harsh words.

No, he wasn't. But he was a way for her to move on, to have a seminormal life, to get her sexual mojo on track. Or to find it. Whatever.

"You don't have to say or do anything but make love to me," Jules assured him.

"Do you need a safe word?" Garrett suggested.

Jules's eyebrows flew up. "A safe word?"

Garrett pushed his hand through his hair, impatient. "In certain situations, a safe word is agreed upon so that if the—"

"What situations?" Jules demanded, trying not to laugh.

"In certain situations when one partner has complete control over the other, a safe word is used when someone is feeling out of their depth—"

"I know how BDSM works, Garrett," Jules told him, trying to hide her smile. "Obviously, I've never indulged." She tipped her head to the side. "Have you?"

He stared at her, completely unembarrassed.

"Once. It wasn't my thing. I prefer more give-and-take in bed, both of us holding equal power."

Jules released a little sigh of relief. She wasn't a prude, and she knew that people enjoyed that kind of stuff, but it wasn't for her. And, honestly, it sounded like a *lot* of work.

"But the thing with a safe word is that it gives you an out, a way to cut through everything to call it quits when the experience becomes overwhelming."

Jules thought about his offer, understood why he was making it and appreciated the gesture. But then she shook her head. "Thanks, but I think we're good. I know I can tell you to stop and that you will."

Something flashed in his eyes that she couldn't identify, something warm and deep and wonderful. Her trust pleased him, she realized. And then Garrett ran the edge of his thumb down her jaw. "Okay, no safe word. I've got the gist of your fear but will you tell me all of it, sometime?"

"I'll try," Jules replied. "And will you tell me what caused you to stand me up in Portland?"

Garrett's thumb tapped against her jaw. "Maybe."

She wanted to ask for more but knew she couldn't. His small concession was enough for now.

"Take me to bed," Jules asked him, holding out her hand.

It was such a simple phrase, one that women used all over the world in different ways and languages, but they both knew that, this time, it held a deeper meaning.

It was a bridge to cross, a new start, the destruction of an old demon.

It meant more.

And Jules was terrified that Garrett did, too.

On Sunday morning, Garrett walked up two flights of stairs carrying an overloaded tray, which contained the biggest coffee carafe he could find—he needed more than one cup to get his brain to work—two big mugs and a box of doughnuts he'd found at the back of the fridge.

Because he was a guy, he figured that if he couldn't see mold growing on them, they had to be edible.

Kicking open the door, he immediately noticed that in the short time he'd been downstairs, Jules had pulled on an oversize sweatshirt and finger-combed her hair. She sat curled up in the bay window, her feet up on the long cushion, staring out over the snow-covered fields. The sun was out, the wind had died down, and the sky was stunningly blue.

He wasn't anxious to get home, despite there being a million Kaye Capital tasks he should be tackling. He also needed to think about James's offer and the role, if any, he was going to play in Ryder International.

He should be listing the pros and cons of having half sisters, a stepmother, the drama that would accompany the announcement that he was James's son. Did he want the burden of inheriting all of Callum's wealth, the shares in the company, being responsible for carrying forward the Ryder name? He wasn't a Ryder, hadn't been for thirty-five years, and probably would never feel like one. He owed them nothing...

But the chance of being part of a family, of spending Christmases and Thanksgivings together, birthdays and pool parties, was an annoying dream that wouldn't completely dissipate, no matter how hard he tried to force the images away. As a child, he'd always wanted a big family but quickly learned that you frequently didn't get the things you most wanted.

Hell, he'd barely had a mother. A family was beyond all possibility.

If he outed himself as a Ryder-White by birth, the most likely outcome was that Tinsley and Kinga would hate him, Penelope would, at best, be wary of him, and James would kill himself trying to make them all happy. Garrett had no idea how Callum would react. No, it wasn't worth it. He was better off alone.

"Coffee's getting cold, Kaye," Jules told him.

He jerked his head up and realized that he'd stopped just inside the room and was staring at nothing. He never lost focus. Annoyed with himself, Garrett placed the tray on the bench at the end of the bed and poured coffee into one of the mugs. He doctored the coffee with cream and handed it to Jules before picking up his cup of black.

Yeah, a good cup of coffee and an excellent view—of woman and scenery—were a great way to start the day.

He could take today, Garrett told himself. Tomorrow was Monday, and he had to get back to Portland and make some decisions, either to keep his world as it was or to flip it on its head. The first was safer, the second more exciting, more tempting.

But temptation frequently came back to bite him in the ass, so he'd go for safe, for what he knew. He was dealing with people, not companies, and humans were inherently unpredictable. With them, it was always better to take the path of least resistance.

But sometimes it was damn boring.

"Sit down, Garrett," Jules softly commanded him.

Garrett sat on the opposite side of the bench, leaned into the wall and placed his feet on either side of Jules's hips. He rested his cup on his thigh and looked at her. The sweatshirt hit her knees and, hopefully, she was still bare-ass naked underneath. She seemed okay, he thought. There had been a few minutes last night when he suspected that she wanted to bolt—not from him but the room—but every time that happened, he dialed up the passion, trying to make her forget where she was, to remind her that the only thing she needed to focus on was him. It had worked.

But he thought he should check, just to make sure. Assumptions were not always accurate. "Are you okay?"

She looked at the rumpled bed, the pillows on the floor and smiled. "Yeah, I'm good."

"And did I cure you of your bedroom phobia?"

She smiled at his deliberately cocky comment.

"You banished some demons. Send me your bill," she flippantly instructed him.

"Honey, you can't afford me," Garrett said with an easy grin.

Jules held her mug to her chest and tipped her head to the side. "It seems that I am the one doing all the talking, Kaye, all the time. How about you telling me something for a change?"

He rolled his shoulders, trying to ease the tension. "I don't like talking about myself, Jules."

"I don't like vegetables, but I eat them because they are good for me," Jules replied, not backing down. "Talk to me, Garrett."

He didn't want to. This extraordinary woman, who'd already slipped under his skin, would make inroads into his heart, and he couldn't let her do that. His heart had to remain impenetrable, its many barriers intact. All his life he'd felt like he was a problem to be solved, and he couldn't bear it if Jules looked at him the same way. He was fine on his own, always had been, always would be.

"It's not healthy to keep everything bottled up inside," Jules told him, sending him a self-deprecating smile. "If you don't talk about it, deal with it, you end up being an almost-thirty-year-old virgin with bedroom issues."

Before he could turn the conversation back to her, she spoke again. "What scares you about talking to me, Garrett?"

Everything?

"I'm a vault. If something is told to me in confidence, I never break it." He believed her and knew that he could trust her to keep her mouth shut. And that was a good thing because his family situation was explosive news.

"And us talking doesn't mean that I'm going to suddenly fall in love with you and demand you give me babies."

He slapped a hand against his heart in mock horror. "You're not?"

"I'd like kids, someday, but I'm not sure about marriage, about being legally bound to someone. I certainly never intend to *obey* any man, ever."

"Now, there's a shocker," Garrett drawled jokingly.

"Ha! You laugh, but so many men think they want an equal partnership, yet when it comes down to it, his career always becomes more important than hers. And when the kids come, the woman is forced to compromise her ambition to be the caregiver, while the man's life doesn't change much." Jules waved her hands in the air. "Stop trying to change the subject, Kaye. We were talking about you, not me."

Unfortunately.

She wouldn't give up. She'd harangue him until he told her something. And he wanted to share, he realized. He wanted to bounce James's wild idea off someone. Jules was here, and he trusted her...

They were lovers, but somehow, in an incredibly short space of time, they'd become friends.

Jules plucked the coffee cup out of his hands, walked over to refill it and handed it back to him.

She sat cross-legged in front of him, her jaw resting on her bunched fist, elbows pressed into her knees. Her full attention was on him. "I recently discovered my mom was in her midthirties when she had an affair with a much younger man. He was twelve, thirteen years younger than her. He was completely in love with her, but she didn't love him with the same intensity."

Jules's eyes didn't leave his face.

"He was only twenty-two or twenty-three, and they'd been sneaking around for months. He wanted to come clean, to show the world that they were a couple, but she was terrified she'd lose her job, and, God, she loved her job. She loved her job more than she ever loved me."

He hadn't meant to verbalize that truth, but it rose to the surface and bubbled over. Around Jules, he kept doing things that weren't in his nature: trying to find a way to save her ranch, sleeping with virgins, playing hooky from work, telling her stuff he never told anyone before.

Jules didn't say anything. She just looked at him, empathy in her amazing eyes.

"I'm an afterthought to my mother, a hassle, someone she had to deal with but would rather not have. I'd nag her to tell me who my father was, and she promised to tell me on my tenth birthday. I turned ten, and she promised to tell me when I was thirteen. Then fifteen, and so it went. I'm still not sure what I'm angrier about, her broken promises or her refusal to tell me about my dad. I believed I had a right to know. Was I wrong?"

"I don't think so," Jules softly replied.

"By the time I hit my midteens, my frustration with her was at an all-time high, as was hers with me. We argued about everything. I said the sky was blue, she said it was green. It wasn't…pleasant."

Garrett went on to explain that Emma was Callum's secretary and that he'd met him, heard him sneeze in the sunlight and seen his strange actions with his fingers. As he expected, Jules's eyes widened in shock. "You're Callum Ryder-White's son?"

"That's been my assumption for the longest time."

"Did you confront your mother?" Jules demanded.

"I did, and she denied it, vehemently. Sometime during the argument, she got me to promise that I would never talk about my theory, that I'd never approach Callum for confirmation." He sipped his coffee and scowled. "She's held me to that promise, and I haven't broken it. I don't break promises, Jules, ever."

"Because your mom broke so many promises to you. That's why you wouldn't promise me that you'd save the ranch. Because you didn't know if you could, and you won't make a promise unless you can deliver on it."

"It's a silly thing, but…yeah. In my business, which is cutthroat as hell and can sometimes be shady, I stick to the truth, always. I've lived with lies and obfuscations, and I hate dishonesty. All I have is my word, and, unlike my mom, I must keep it."

"I get it, Garrett. I do."

"It's equally important that the people I care about keep their word," Garrett told her, the warning in his voice unmistakable.

"You either trust me or you don't, Garrett," Jules quietly told him, her expression dignified. "I'm not going to beg you to."

He saw something in her eyes that reassured him, but being cynical, he wondered if he was seeing something that wasn't there because he *wanted* to trust her. It scared him shitless, but it was novel and exciting and felt like he was riding a roller coaster blindfolded.

He was going to tell her. He simply couldn't hold back.

"As I was recently, and reliably, informed, Callum isn't my father," Garrett released the words and opened the door.

Her eyes widened. "And do you know who is?"

He nodded. He bent sideways to put his coffee cup on the floor and bent his legs, resting his arms loosely around his knees. "James came to see me just before I was supposed to join you at that bar."

He remembered James's nervousness, the fear mixed with determination on his face. He hadn't known how Garrett would react, but he'd walked into his office, spine straight and shoulders back, and done what he'd come to do.

Offer Garrett the job as CEO and inform him of his parentage. It had been hard for him, but he'd done it, and Garrett had to admire his resolve.

"Callum is in the hospital, and they are looking for a CEO. James offered me the position, and I laughed in his face. Why would I want to leave my kingdom for a place I don't know and an industry I know next to nothing about?"

"C'mon, Garrett, you have an encyclopedic knowledge of many different industries, and the basics of any business are the same. Buy low, sell high, cover your costs and make a profit. You could run a trading store on Mars if you wanted to."

Her faith in him warmed him. And, yeah, he did have a knack for business, could see trends and anticipate big-picture results. He could run Ryder International. He just didn't want to.

He didn't think.

"You were telling me about James and his CEO offer…" Jules nudged his knee.

Yeah. "I refused him, laughed in his face. He sat down in a chair, crossed his legs and told me, with remarkable sangfroid, that with one word in Callum's ear, he could dump Ryder International in my hands whether I wanted it or not."

Jules lifted her hands, asking for an explanation.

"Callum and James have a very rocky relationship."

Jules nodded. "He treats him like a servant. I don't know why James puts up with Callum."

"Because he's the sole male heir, the last Ryder-White male. Callum won't leave the business to Tinsley or Kinga. They don't carry the necessary equipment."

Fury jumped into Jules's eyes. "The misogynistic bastard."

"Yep." Garrett raked a hand through his hair. "Apparently, Callum informed James that should he become aware of a male son, grandson or nephew, someone else who carries the Ryder-White genes, that man will inherit Callum's wealth, not James. If Callum dies and the executor of the will becomes aware of another Ryder-White, James will be shoved aside in favor of the new heir."

It sounded unbelievable... It was unbelievable.

"But why? What could James have done that Callum would turn on him like that?" Jules asked, shocked.

It was a question he'd asked himself, many times. "I don't know."

Jules's arched eyebrows pulled together. He watched as she worked her way through his words and when her eyes widened, he knew she'd hit on something. "James said that he could dump Ryder's on you whether you wanted it or not."

Garrett nodded.

"Does that mean that you are a son, a grandson or a nephew?" Jules said.

God, she was quick. And he loved her mind, the way it worked. He nodded.

"So which are you, Garrett?"

Garrett inhaled, filling his lungs. "James was the young man who got my mother pregnant. I'm Callum's grandson. My teenage observations weren't that wide of the mark."

Her mouth dropped open, and he could see words forming on her tongue, yet she made no sound. Garrett gripped her chin and pushed her jaw up. He managed a wry smile. "Welcome to my world, Juliana-Jaliyah. In the last two days, I've acquired a father, a stepmother, two sisters and a company. And it's all up to me if I want to acknowledge them. James has handed the decision over to me. I can either acknowledge everything—and run Ryder International—or not. It's my decision."

"Holy hell. What are you going to do?"

"I don't have a freakin' clue."

Nine

Jules finally understood why Garrett had looked so agitated on Friday night. It was a hell of a thing to discover that you were someone's son, and the additional burden of hearing that he held the fate of the Ryder-White family, who were little better than strangers to him, in his hands had to weigh heavily on his mind. Jules knew that Garrett was a loner, self-contained and emotionally independent, so hearing he had a father who wanted to acknowledge him, a stepmother and two half sisters must have made the earth shift below his feet.

With all that going on, why did he head west with her to help someone he didn't know? Who was this man? He was a mass of contradictions—tender and tough, sweet and so smart—and she could spend a lifetime trying to figure him out. She doubted she ever would, but she'd sure like to try.

Wow, Carlson! You barely know the man, and you're making plans... What is wrong with you?

He wasn't her forever guy; she didn't think such a creature existed. And she didn't believe in tying herself—legally—to a man. It was too big a risk, too huge an ask.

She'd seen all the facets of love, and many of them were ugly and violent. She never wanted to run the risk of being caught in that particular trap.

Her heart was convinced he'd never hurt her, that he'd rather die than lift a hand to her, but her brain— suspicious organ that it was—kept reminding her that her father was perfect-husband material before he'd placed a ring on her mom's finger. He first hit her on their honeymoon, before the ink on their marriage certificate was dry.

Her father had fooled so many people: his friends, his family, his work colleagues. At a very young age, Jules promised herself that she'd always remain alert, that she'd never allow herself to fall in love, to hand a man enough power to hurt her, physically *and* emotionally...

But, damn, Garrett tempted her to do exactly that. She'd listen to her brain, thank you very much...

But her body was demanding another bout of bed-based fun. If she'd known that sex was this much fun, she'd have pushed herself to get over her little phobia sooner.

She twisted her lips. No, she wouldn't have... It

had taken Garrett striding into her life for her to face her fears. She wanted him more than she wanted to hold on to the safety her issues afforded her. Jules looked out the window, squinting against the bright sunlight. The snow, which was less heavy than expected, would melt fast, and if memory served her correctly, by this afternoon the roads would be navigable. She had, maybe, half a day left with Garrett, and she intended to make the most of it.

And while she indulged, she'd hopefully banish some of his blues, too.

Jules placed her hand on his knees to push them down and then straddled his thick thighs and lowered her head to allow her lips to meet his. She felt his smile against her lips, full of sunlight, and kissed the corner of his mouth. Garrett allowed her to play, his hands coming to rest lightly on her hips under her sweatshirt. She blushed as his hand swept over the curve of her bare buttock, embarrassed that she hadn't pulled on any underwear.

Then again, she loved her pretty bras and gossamer-thin panties and paid a fortune for them. She couldn't afford to replace more ripped-away underwear.

"You are so lovely, Juliana," Garrett murmured, as his fingers dug into the skin on her lower back. "Being here, with you, has been a step out of time, a lovely distraction."

Jules frowned. She didn't want to be a distraction; she wanted to be a necessity... *No!* What was she thinking? This interlude with Garrett was exactly that: a blip, a never-to-be-repeated weekend. She couldn't allow herself to get emotional or sentimental. She had to be practical.

"You stopped kissing me—" Garrett spoke against her lips "—and I miss your mouth."

Jules gave herself a mental slap and lowered her lips back to his, telling herself to enjoy him, that she was running out of time to kiss and touch this gorgeous man. Shuddering, she slipped her tongue inside his mouth, allowing passion to swamp her.

She wanted to stop thinking and start feeling, to leave her head and be immersed in the scent, taste and feel of him. She wanted hot and hard and fast, for him to brand her, to burn away her thoughts of fidelity and forever.

Garrett gripped the side of her face in his long, gentle fingers and pushed her back to look into her eyes. "Slow down, baby, I want to savor this. I want to savor you."

No, soft and sweet would rip her apart, and she wasn't sure if she'd be able to cobble herself back together. Jules turned her head and bit his thumb. "I want hot and fast and out of control. Think you can manage that, Kaye?"

He was a guy and, like all alpha men, couldn't resist a challenge. His eyes narrowed, and the glint in those blue depths tempted her. "Are you sure you can handle that, Jules?"

Hell, she never backed down from a challenge, either. He lifted her chin, and she returned his challenging stare. "I can take anything you dish out, Garrett. I'm not a fragile flower."

"No, you're not," Garrett said, dropping his hands to grip her hips. He lifted her off him and deposited her on the edge of the bench, before dropping to his knees in front of her. He spread her legs, looked at her and sat down on the floor, crossing his legs. He placed his hands on his knees and sent her a wicked, wicked smile.

"You're already wet… That's so hot, Jules. Bet I can make you come without me touching you at all."

Yeah, she didn't think so. Jules shook her head. "Contrary to what you've heard, Garrett Kaye, you're good, but you're not that good."

Garrett just smiled. "Take off your sweatshirt, baby."

Jules wanted to demand that he come up and do it himself, but his dark eyes asked her to trust him, to play this game with him. To make this memory…

She slowly lifted her sweatshirt, exposing the skin at the top of her thighs, her stomach, her rib cage and her breasts. Then she deliberately dropped the shirt and started the process again, enjoying the way Garrett's eyes turned to molten teal.

"Tease," Garrett murmured.

"But you like it," Jules replied, finally tossing her shirt to the floor. He picked it up, buried his nose in its folds and inhaled.

"You smell so damn good. You always do," Garrett told her, placing his hands on the floor behind him and stretching out his long legs. He looked at her feet and slowly made his way up her body, stopping to stare at her feminine folds. Jules, feeling exposed, fought the urge to close her legs, but the appreciation in his eyes kept her knees apart, and she felt a low throb pulse at the edge of her womb.

He was right. This was hot.

"Touch your breast, Jules. Roll your nipples through your fingers," Garrett commanded her.

Jules did as he ordered and then stopped, frowning. "Hey, you said you can make *me* come without any touching! This is cheating."

"No, I said I can make you come without *me* touching *you*." He grinned. "Always read the fine print, darling. Touch yourself, Jules. Feel your marvelous skin, the texture of your nipples, the curve of your breasts."

Jules closed her eyes, lost in his deep voice, the sensations he pulled to the surface. She was so hot, so turned on, and when he told her to run her hand across her stomach, she was eager to follow his order. Her hand dipped down, and he shook his head.

"I didn't say you could do that."

Jules pulled her hand back and allowed her gaze to drift over him. His eyes blazed with barely harnessed desire, and a muscle ticked in his jaw. He held himself rigid, as if he were forcing himself not to reach for her, all leashed power and masculine grace. Her eyes drifted over his T-shirt-clad chest, over his flat stomach. His erection pushed the thin fabric of his sweatpants up, showing her exactly how much he wanted her.

And that was a lot.

Jules felt her pleasure build, knew that if she touched herself, she'd come. "I need—"

"I know exactly what you need," Garrett growled. "Push your hands between your legs, down your thighs, but don't touch yourself."

So near but so far. Jules rested the back of her head against the windowpane and stared up at the ceiling, not caring that she was utterly, incredibly exposed to Garrett. He could see every part of her, and she didn't care.

She just wanted all the pleasure he could give her.

"You're so sexy, Juliana. I'm so hard for you."

"Are you touching yourself?" Jules asked, her eyes still closed.

"No. Are you close, Ju?"

"So close," Jules whispered. "I want—"

"What do you want, baby?"

"To fly," she whispered.

"Then do it. Come now, sweetheart, come for me."

Jules didn't hesitate, her fingers finding her sweet spot, and with one swipe, two, she shuddered and tipped over into that abyss of pleasure. She screamed and shuddered, clamping her thighs together against her hand, drawing the pleasure out.

When her shudders calmed down to the occasional tremor, she opened her eyes to see Garrett watching her. She couldn't help her fierce blush, embarrassed at her screams and that she'd forgotten he was there.

"Sexiest thing I've ever seen," Garrett told her. He

stood up slowly and held out his hand. Jules slid her palm into his and allowed him to pull her to her feet.

"Come back to bed with me, baby."

Jules nodded, knowing that when he looked at her like that—like she had hung the moon and stars—she'd follow him wherever he wanted to go.

Literally a minute after he exploded inside her, Jules heard Kate's melodious voice floating up the stairs.

"We're back! Get your lazy asses out of bed."

Garrett groaned, rolled off her onto his back and slapped his forearm over his eyes. The door was open, they hadn't been quiet, and ten minutes ago Jules had been plastered against the bay window, naked and exposed.

"Am I going to be met with the business end of a shotgun when I walk down the stairs?"

Jules knew that Kate and Peta were probably doing a happy dance downstairs at the thought of Jules having a man in her bed—*Sex is natural and a great way to relieve stress, darling*—but couldn't help teasing Garrett, just a little.

"Maybe," she told him.

"Awesome," Garrett dryly muttered. "Maybe exiting the house via the third-story window is a reasonable option."

She grinned at him as she shoved back the covers and stood up. She picked up a throw lying on the end of the bed, wrapped it around herself and walked over to the open door. She slammed it closed and moved back to the window and sighed at the cold, clear day. The mountains were in-your-face close, and the sky was a sharp blue. Gorgeous, she thought.

Judging by Kate and Peta's return, the roads were navigable, and she had to think about leaving Kilconnell Ranch. She was flying to Cancun soon, and from there she was heading to Montego Bay.

She'd only return to the States in three weeks.

The thought did not excite her.

But it was her job and a well-paying one. Garrett hadn't found anything in Kate's books that would suggest a way out of her financial woes, so she'd be supporting Kate and Peta for the foreseeable future. To do that she needed to earn more, and that meant increasing her workload. She'd have to look at doing more TV and cooking shows, endorsements, demonstrations.

She wouldn't have time for a lover or even a fling. And dropping in and out of Garrett's life would be like repeatedly stabbing herself between the eyes with a rusty fork. Seeing him again would be a high, sex would take her higher, and leaving him would drop her like a sack of concrete.

And if she fell in love with him—and that was a distinct possibility—those highs and lows would increase exponentially. She needed to be emotionally upbeat to do her job, and she couldn't see how she'd feel anything but miserable when she was away from him.

No, it was better to call it quits, while she still could. She turned to look at him and opened her mouth to speak, and her words caught in her throat. With his hand tucked behind his head, he looked relaxed and lazy, satisfied. And years younger than the tense man who'd stepped off the plane yesterday.

She'd give him—them—a few more hours. She'd tell him in Portland.

"Is there anything at all you can do about Kate and saving her ranch?" she asked.

Garrett sighed, flung back the covers and walked over to his clothes, yanking on his sweatpants. They rode low on his hips and showed off his sexy hip muscles and Jules felt that now-familiar surge of heat and need. She'd just had a series of orgasms, and she wanted him again!

She needed to change the subject and get confirmation of her suspicions. "So what's your final diagnosis on Crazy Kate's state of health?"

"I didn't find anything that would help the situation, Jules," Garrett bluntly told her.

Jules sat down on the edge of the bed, feeling like he'd gut punched her. "Nothing at all?"

"She needs thirty million to cover her debts, to pull herself out of the hole she's in. This place is only worth five to seven million, on a good day. So unless she finds thirty mil in the next two weeks, she's going to lose her shirt no matter what."

Jules gripped the bridge of her nose, blinking away hot tears. "So there's nothing she can do?"

Garrett lifted his powerful shoulder. "Unless she has a secret stash of shares or an investment she's forgotten about, and it would have to be a hell of a honeypot, then it's over, Jules."

Jules frowned, his words pulling up a vague memory. She scratched her forehead, trying to grab hold of it.

"What is it, Jules?"

Jules looked at him, frowning. "Her husband was a speculator, he played the stock market. He bought a lot of speculative shares."

"When he died, those shares would've passed to Kate, and they would've been included in his estate. I'm sure the accountants would've found them. I understand that you are clutching at straws but—"

"I need to know that I've done everything I can. I can't have any regrets, Garrett. I want to be able to say that I did everything I could. How do I check?"

Garrett rubbed the back of his neck. "I can get one of my people to search, but it would help if we knew what we were looking for. Does Kate still have the computer he used?"

"Yeah, in the study. It's in the cupboard." Jules winced. "It's pretty old. I don't know if it still works."

"I'll ask Kate if I can take the hard drive, and I'll get my PA working on it. He knows his way around computers."

"Thank you," she quietly stated, allowing her turbulent emotions to coat her words. "Thank you for coming with me, for trying to help Kate, for introducing me to amazing sex. For this weekend."

Her eyes slammed into his, and she held her breath as his fingers skimmed her cheek, her lips. His eyes were a soft teal, tender as hell, and she sucked in her breath. If there was anyone in the world she could trust completely, it was Garrett.

However much she was tempted, she refused to allow that to happen.

"Breakfast is ready. Get down here!" Kate yelled, breaking the tension between them.

"I'll use my en suite bathroom to shower," Garrett told her, standing up. He scooped up his T-shirt and pulled it over his head in an economical movement. "I'll see you downstairs."

Jules nodded.

"I'd like to leave in a couple of hours. Does that suit you?"

Jules forced herself to nod. Their lovely, out-of-step weekend was over, and it was time to go back to reality.

She wanted to stay here, with him. Going back to reality didn't hold any appeal, at all.

When they arrived at the airport, his Bentley Bentayga, as per his instructions, was waiting for him in the pickup zone. He threw their bags into the trunk, helped Jules into the passenger seat and slid behind the wheel, settling into the super luxurious leather seats. Pulling into the traffic, he glanced at Jules, saw that she was looking out the window and sighed at her remote expression. They'd eaten a late breakfast with Kate and Peta, and she'd made an effort to be sociable, but on the drive to the airport and the flight back home, she'd barely spoken. His gregarious girl was gone, and a sophisticated stranger had taken her place.

It was odd. He normally liked stylish, quiet women, but he didn't like the look on Jules. She was energetic and vivacious, wide smiles and warmth. Playing it cool didn't suit her.

"I need directions on where to take you," Garrett told her, as he pulled into traffic. The next words escaped before he could pull them back. "Or you can just come back to my place."

Jules plugged her address into the onboard GPS—the car's computer could power a spaceship—and shook her head. "I thought we agreed that we weren't looking for anything permanent, Kaye."

"It was an offer for you to come back to my place, not an invitation to move in," Garrett replied, keeping his voice mild. The fact that she didn't want to extend their time together hurt him, far more than it should.

What the hell?

Jules half turned in her seat, and he saw the frustration on her face. "Okay, say I come home with you and spend the night? The day after tomorrow I'm flying to Cancun, from there I'm off to Jamaica. I'm not going to be home for three weeks."

"So, I'll see you in three weeks, then."

Jules looked irritated. "And then what? We carry on sleeping together?"

Sleeping, laughing, talking… He was up for any and all of it.

Garrett checked his mirrors and moved over a lane. "Would that be a problem?"

"Maybe not for you, but it would for me. I'm not cut out—I don't think—for a no-strings affair. Neither can I commit to anyone, so I'm stuck in this weird place, a no-man's-land." Jules pushed a curl behind her ear.

He hadn't wanted anything more than to sleep with her, but sometime over the last thirty-six hours, that had changed. He didn't want to let her go, couldn't allow her to walk out of his life, not just yet. He didn't know where this was going, how it would pan out, but the thought of never seeing her again, hearing her laugh, tasting her smile, talking to her, was not something he was prepared to accept.

"What if I said that we should see where this went, how it could grow?" Shit, what was he saying? Was he really prepared to consider a relationship with this woman, someone who buzzed around the world like a bee on steroids? He'd never see her, would have minimal time with her, and he'd be constantly saying goodbye.

But anything would be better than nothing. Of that, he was convinced.

"I'm not what you want, Garrett."

The finality in her words, her complete conviction, annoyed him. "I'm thirty-five years old. Do not tell me how I feel."

Jules threw her hands up in the air. "I can't, Garrett. I have to walk away from you, now, *today*."

He banged his hand against the leather steering wheel. "Why?"

"Because if I don't, I'll fall for you, and I can't do that. I can't be with anyone like that. I can't give that much of myself, and I will never be a man's possession."

"I've never treated a woman like my possession, *ever*. I don't believe in that shit."

"That's what my mom believed about my dad, and look how well that turned out!" Jules shouted.

Garrett slapped his hand against the leather steering wheel again. "I am not your goddamn father! I would never, ever hurt you." Jesus, they shouldn't be having this conversation while driving; he needed to concentrate.

Jules's curls bounced. "My heart knows that, but my brain won't get with the program. My brain thinks it's better, safer, to be free, to be unattached. Attachment equals hurt. Staying in one place, with one person, means I'll be trapped. I can't be trapped, Garrett."

"I'm not going to lock you in a goddamn cage, Jules! I just want to be able to see you, talk to you, make sure you're okay, enjoy your fabulous body. For you to enjoy me."

"But in no time at all, I'd find myself emotionally trapped."

She was scared, Garrett realized, terrified of repeating her mom's mistakes. He understood that, could even empathize, but she was throwing away something incredible, an amazing connection, because she was scared. That was unacceptable.

"Stop being a wuss and trust yourself, Carlson!" he snapped. "You're being a coward."

He glanced at her, saw the anger flare in her eyes and jerked his eyes back to the road. He was expecting an eruption and was surprised when she spoke in a calm, measured tone.

"Aren't we all scared, Garrett? Even you?"

He frowned. "What do I have to be scared about?"

Sure, he was a little concerned that he might drop to his knees, throw his arms around her legs and beg her not to leave, but apart from that…nothing much affected him.

"You're terrified of acknowledging that you are James's son because you'll have to deal with the drama of having a new family, of disappointing your mother. You'll have to deal with all those pesky people and their emotions. It's far, far easier to walk away than embrace a new reality."

Her words hit him like poison-tipped arrows, piercing his skin and setting his cells on fire. He didn't want to acknowledge the truth of her statement, that every time he thought about the Ryder-Whites, he imagined Sunday lunches, catching a game with James, teasing his sisters, playing pickup and trash-talking with their guys, enjoying family holidays at one of his many, never-used vacation homes.

He wanted that. Wanted it so much it hurt to breathe.

But that was a dream, a mirage, a bubble that would immediately burst as soon as he reached for it. No, it was far more realistic to assume that any relationship with James would be a minefield, that Tinsley and Kinga would resent him, that Penelope would hate him.

Besides, where would he find the time for a family? Kaye Capital already took up all hours of the day. His lack of time was a valid excuse. "I have enough on my plate without taking on the running of a massive, international company, Jules!"

"You wouldn't have to run it on a day-to-day basis, and you know that. They have excellent people, and with James there, you'd only have to make the big-picture decisions. Running Ryder International isn't the issue, as you well know! What terrifies you is having a father, sisters, people to care for you."

"You're assuming that Kinga and Tinsley would even like a brother!" Garrett retorted. He liked them. Admired their strength and work ethic and obvious intelligence and would be proud to call them his sisters. But the reverse might not be true. He had a reputation in the business world for being a bastard, and they'd resent him for horning in on their inheritance, on their lives. They were Ryder-Whites. He wasn't. He just carried James's genes.

And Callum's. God help him.

"The Ryder-Whites are nice people, Garrett. You should give them a chance."

"Stop, Jules! Look, this is my problem, and I'll deal with them," Garrett shouted, frustrated. They'd been talking about their relationship—or

nonrelationship, whatever the hell they had or didn't
have—not about his family.

"If you hurt them, Kinga and Tinsley specifically,
I'll never forgive you."

Her words sucker punched him, and the impact
was followed by searing pain, a mental kick in the
head. She was so ready to defend them, to fight for
them but not for him. She wasn't worried about how
he'd come through this situation, how he'd feel. Her
friends were a priority; he wasn't. He was just the
guy who introduced her to sex.

It had always been like this. He was expected to
deal with his shit in his own way. On his own. Nobody, not even his mother, had ever been prepared
to stand in his corner and fight for him, protect him.

He was alone. And Jules was telling him that was
the way it would always be.

To hell with her. To hell with them all! He didn't
need Jules. He knew a dozen women he could hook
up with at a moment's notice, and he had his own
business to run, the business he'd built without any
help from anyone.

That wasn't true. He'd had the money from the
trust James had set up for him, and he'd used that
cash as the building blocks of his business. He owed
him for that.

That could be easily rectified. He'd repay James
his money and tell him that he wasn't interested
in having anything to do with him or Ryder International. He'd drop off Jules and put her, and this
weekend, out of his mind. He was giving too much

importance to a two-day fling. He'd forget that he had sisters and that he was part of, genetically at least, the Ryder-White clan.

As he knew, connecting and then being rejected hurt like hell, and he was better on his own. Tough, hard-assed, self-reliant.

Put a fork in him. He was done.

Ten

Garrett heard Sven's knock on his office door and hastily minimized Jules's Instagram account. But the photograph of her, dressed in a flame-orange bikini top and a matching patterned sarong knotted low on her hips, standing next to a beach bar, was burned into his brain.

He'd licked that belly button, traced the curve of those fabulous breasts with his tongue, kissed that wide, smiling mouth.

How dare she look so happy when he was as surly as sin?

"What?" Garrett looked up when Sven cleared his throat.

Sven sent him a steady look and lifted one pierced

eyebrow. "Do you know how long this mood of yours is going to last?" he politely inquired.

Garrett glared at him. "I am not in a mood!"

Garrett glanced at the window and waited for the bolt of lightning to hit him for verbalizing that whopper. When it didn't, he felt vaguely disappointed. "What's it to you, anyway?" Garrett demanded.

Sven shrugged. "Well, if you are going to mope around for another week or two, I might be able to get through it without stabbing you. Any longer than that and I might end up in jail," Sven mused.

Garrett winced, silently acknowledging the point. Since returning from Colorado, he'd been in a foul mood. He couldn't concentrate, was barely eating and hadn't exercised since Jules left a week ago.

He'd spent a day and a bit with her, and he was acting like a lovesick fool. God, he was pathetic.

Garrett spun his chair around and stared at the boats bobbing in Portland's harbor. He shouldn't be missing her this much. There was no rhyme or reason for it. He'd spent one night with her...

And they hadn't done much sleeping.

But she knew him better than anyone else in the world, and he knew her secrets—secrets she'd never shared with her best friends. With Jules, he felt better, calmer, more relaxed, easier to be with, simply nicer.

But Jules was ten, twelve, hours away on a goddamn beach, and he hadn't had any contact with her in ten days. That was nine days and twenty-three hours too long.

Was she okay? Working too hard? Sleeping with someone else?

Garrett gritted his teeth, and he imagined flecks of enamel hitting the inside of his cheeks. He couldn't stand it, being away from her, but what choice did he have? She didn't want him in her life.

"I came to tell you that I found something on that hard drive you wanted me to investigate," Sven said.

What hard drive? What was he talking about? Garrett spun around and asked for an explanation.

"The hard drive you brought back from Colorado with a 'See if you find anything interesting on this hard drive'?"

Right. The hard drive he'd taken from Kate's husband's computer. Garrett placed his forearms on his desk and nodded. "Okay, I'm following you... What did you find? And no, porn isn't interesting."

Sven smiled at his weak joke. "I found a lot of financial documents on the drive. Whoever owned the laptop was a hell of a businessman."

Yeah, he knew that. "He left Kate a ton of money, and that's how she financed the reopening and expansion of Crazy Kate's."

"I found share certificates and a list of bank accounts. But upon further investigation, they all became part of his estate when he died."

Not a surprise, Garrett thought. "So, what else did you find?"

"Bitcoin."

Of everything that he'd expected Sven to say, that

wasn't the sentence he expected to hear. "Bullshit," Garrett said.

Sven grinned. "I know, it sounds improbable, right? I mean, there are so many urban legends out there about people who find old computers with Bitcoin stashed on them, but they are all BS. It never happens."

"But there's cryptocurrency on that computer?" he asked, excitement coursing through his system.

"There's a wallet, but without looking inside it, I can't tell if he owned any crypto."

"So look inside it," Garrett told him. "Do you need a code?"

Sven looked insulted. "I was hacking computer wallets when I was a kid, so no, I don't need a code."

"Excellent." Garrett pushed his chair back and walked to the door. "Let's go look and see what's in the wallet. I'm not getting my hopes up. It's probably nothing. Up until relatively recently crypto was an obscure concept and few people knew about it. Here's hoping Kate's husband knew about the digital currency early on."

"Only one way to find out," Sven said.

In his office, Sven sat behind his messy desk and, with fingers flying across the keyboard, brought up an old-fashioned screen filled with icons. Sven pointed to the wallet, and Garrett's heart thumped in his chest. He couldn't make Jules happy, love her for the rest of her life or give her security and stability and babies, but maybe he could save Kate's beloved ranch for her.

You're getting your hopes up, Kaye. This is a million-to-zero long shot.

The screen went black, Sven's fingers danced on the keyboard, and code rolled across the screen. He issued a satisfied grunt and stared at the code for a minute before switching back and opening the wallet.

A log-in screen appeared, and Sven punched in the twelve-digit alphanumeric code from memory. The screen changed, and Garrett stared at the figures on the screen.

"Does that say that there is crypto worth more than forty million?" Garrett asked, his voice coming from a place far, far away.

"Forty-two million to be precise," Sven said, leaning back in his chair, a satisfied grin on his face.

"Holy shit," Garrett said, looking at the screen again, just to confirm. That was more than enough to pay off the bulk of Kate's debts and, most importantly, save Kilconnell Ranch.

Garrett gripped Sven's shoulder with a shaking hand. "I need to get to Colorado, so get my pilot to file a flight plan. I'll leave for the airport immediately."

Sven nodded and reached for his phone.

"And disconnect the hard drive. I'm taking it with me," he added.

He could call Kate, but he preferred to tell them this momentous news in person. And being with the people Jules loved most made him feel closer to her.

What a sap.

"I would, and I could, but James Ryder-White will be here in five minutes," Sven stated.

Garrett stared at him. God, he couldn't cope with his biological father at the moment, didn't want to. He'd tell James that he was uninterested in running Ryder International when he returned from Colorado.

"Call him and cancel," Garrett told Sven.

"I'm already here."

Garrett spun around to see James standing in the doorway to Sven's office, the Kaye Capital receptionist at his elbow. Crap. Oh, well, he could give the guy a few minutes.

How long would it take to get James to understand that he wasn't interested? Two minutes? Three?

Garrett gestured to James to follow him. He'd get this done and then head to the Rockies. Saving Kate's company and the ranch was far more important than anything James had to say.

"He's with someone at the moment," a tired-looking nurse told Garrett when he asked to see Callum Ryder-White.

Garrett suspected he knew who Callum's visitor was. "Slim woman, platinum-blond hair?"

The nurse nodded. "My mother," Garrett explained. "She works as his assistant."

Short on sleep and just in from Colorado—with Kate's and Peta's screams of joy and relief still ringing in his ears—he didn't have any patience for bureaucracy so he stared the nurse down. She eventually nodded, gave him directions to Callum's room and admonished him to not stay long. Garrett jammed his hands in the pockets of his chinos and walked down the long corridor, the smell of antiseptic tickling his nose. A doctor brushed past him— young, pretty and female—but all her concentration was on her clipboard, and he could've been a fly on the wall for all she noticed.

It didn't bother him in the least. There was only one woman whose attention he needed, and she was in Montego Bay, making cocktails on a freakin' beach.

He'd lost her, but having had Jules in his life, even so brief a time, made him realize that he didn't want to live a solitary life. It was time to accept that he needed people in his life, as messy as they made it. He needed his rough edges, and his spikes, rubbed off, his views tempered and challenged. He became a better person around people, was at his best with Jules.

But if he was going to be less antisocial, then he might as well start with the people who were related to him. James, Kinga and Tinsley…

But not with his grandfather; he didn't see them having a relationship. James had already told him that if you weren't for Callum, then you were against him. And he'd already chosen to join Team James.

Do not lose your temper with Callum, Garrett reminded himself. *Or your mother.*

Garrett rapped on the door and heard his mom's voice telling him to come in. He stepped inside the room and looked around. It looked nothing like a normal, sterile hospital room. Callum's bed was covered in expensive linen, a huge bouquet of lilies sat in a vase, and two laptops sat on a small table in the corner. There were crystal glasses on the bedside table, and a cashmere blanket lay across the end of Callum's bed.

Emma frowned at him. "Garrett, this is a surprise."

She had no idea. And he had a lot more of those up his sleeve.

He looked from his mom's puzzled face to Callum's cool one and walked over to where the man sat, his hand outstretched. Callum's grip was frail, and the old man looked terrible, Garrett decided. Gaunt and washed-out, a shell of who he'd been at the Valentine's Day Ball.

"I'm afraid we don't have another chair for you," Callum said, as his mom sat down at the table opposite Callum.

"That's fine. I'm not going to take up too much of your time."

Callum's sharp eyes rested on his face. "Why are you here? Your mother might work for me, but our paths have never crossed."

He wasn't surprised that Callum didn't remember their previous meeting. Garrett walked over to the wall and pushed his right shoulder into it, deliberately keeping his posture relaxed.

"You tasked James with finding Ryder International a CEO," Garrett stated. He heard his mom's sharp inhale and, out of the corner of his eye, saw her face pale.

"I did, and he's been, as he always does, dragging his feet," Callum snapped. He gestured to the pile of paper next to his elbows. "Emma and I are working through the résumés."

"James offered me the position," Garrett informed them. Callum's eyes narrowed, and his mom released another low, shocked gasp.

"Why?" Emma asked, in a shaky voice. Garrett met her eyes, thinking she looked old and more than a little scared.

"You know why, Mom."

"He told you?"

"Yeah, he did. And it was something you should've done a long, long time ago. You had no right to keep his identity from me, keep him from me."

"I did what I thought was best," Emma protested.

"No, you did what was best for your career," Garrett countered. "You were worried that if Callum found out who made you pregnant, you might lose your job. Or that they'd take me away from you. But I think you were more concerned about your career than your child."

"That's not fair," Emma whispered.

"He wanted to be my dad. He wanted to acknowledge me, be in my life. But you made that impossible," Garrett stated, his voice hard.

Emma's hands bunched into tight fists. "Did he tell you what I did to make him back off?"

"No, but judging from your petrified expression, it must've been a pretty shitty card you played."

Callum's hand slapping the table brought Garrett's

attention back to him. "What are you talking about? What are you saying?"

Here goes, Garrett thought.

"James and Emma had an affair before he was married. I am a result of that affair. I am James's son and your grandson." Garrett pushed a hand through his hair. "God help me."

Callum stared at him for a long time before lifting a bony finger and pointing it at his face. "You will have a DNA test to prove that you are related to me," Callum said, his hand shaking. "When that test comes back positive, I will continue this conversation with you."

Garrett rolled his eyes. "Emma isn't disputing that James is my father, you and I both sneeze when we walk into the sunlight, and Jesus, I look exactly like you did when you were young. But sure, let's put your mind at ease with a DNA test."

Callum stared at him, and Garrett knew his mind was going a mile a minute, no doubt trying to work out how to turn this to his advantage. When Callum started to speak, he held up his hand. "No, Callum, you're not calling the shots. Not today, and never with me."

"But—"

"Today you are going to listen," Garrett told him. He stood up straight and folded his arms across his torso, thinking that he was so tired. But more than sleep, what he wanted to do was lay eyes on Jules. Enfold her in his arms, bury his nose in her sweet-smelling curls.

But for that to happen, Jules had to trust him, and he didn't think she would. Not him or any other man.

Garrett pulled his attention back to his mother and grandfather. "James has an emergency power of attorney, one the lawyers kept on file in case you were ever incapacitated. Using that power of attorney, James hired me as a CEO-slash-consultant to Ryder International. He will be making the day-to-day decisions and calling on me, and Tinsley and Kinga, for help with the bigger decisions."

"I am not happy with that," Callum blustered.

"Well, the board is, including the representative of the person or entity holding the huge block of shares not owned by Ryder-White."

"Do you know who owns those shares? I want to buy them!"

James had told him that Callum was obsessed with getting those shares back under his control, that they'd once belonged to his brother Ben but had passed out of the family's hands.

"Who owns those shares is not important right now, Callum," Emma told him, patting his hand. Garrett saw the affection in her eyes… No, it was more than affection: it was love. She loved and adored Callum. Had James just been a substitute for the man she could never have?

Possibly. It was something to think about.

"James told me that if you ever found another close male relative, you'd write him out of your will. That's a pretty crappy thing to do."

"He sided with my brother over me," Callum immediately responded. "I promised him he'd pay for it someday."

Really? Hadn't that happened nearly forty years ago? What a waste of energy. And if Garrett continued to argue with Callum, he'd be wasting his. No, it was better to focus on the issue at hand.

"Once I have concrete proof, DNA proof, I will leave everything to you, but only if you change your name to Ryder-White," Callum stated.

God, the old man was stubborn. "I have no plans to change my name. James doesn't care one way or the other, and it's his opinion I value. As for your will…"

Callum cocked his head when Garrett hesitated.

He waited a few more beats before handing his grandfather a cold smile. "You can take your will and shove it, Callum. I don't need your money, your influence or your possessions. I don't need a damn thing from you." He only needed Jules, standing by his side, walking through life with him. But if she couldn't trust him, what was the point?

Callum's jaw dropped open, shock flashing across his face. "What?"

"And if you decide to leave everything to me, the first thing I will do is instruct my lawyers to divide it three ways, with your son and your granddaughters getting an equal share. Personally, I think you should leave it to James—he's earned every cent of it—but if you can't wrap your stubborn brain around that concept and you do leave it to me, I promise you that's what will happen."

"You can't do that!" Callum shouted. "I can put a clause in that will stop you from doing that."

"Okay, do that. But then I will run the company into the ground, strip it out and sell it off. The proceeds will be split between my father and my half sisters. Those are your options, Callum, and I suggest you choose carefully."

He'd backed him into a corner, and Callum knew it. He glared at Garrett, spit forming in the corners of his mouth. "I don't think I like you, Kaye."

Garrett's lips lifted in a small smile. "That's okay, I know I don't like you." He looked at his mom, who hadn't yet managed to pull her eyes off him.

"You really should've told me, Mom."

She nodded, devastation in her eyes. "I know. Can we talk again?"

Along with needing people, he also needed a dad. He'd missed out on thirty-plus years of having a father and that was long enough. His mom's actions were inconceivable. "You kept my dad from me, a person I needed, who wanted to be part of my life. That's pretty harsh and unforgivable." He lifted his shoulders, and when they fell, he felt a hundred years old. "I don't know about talking, I really don't. I'll let you know when I figure it out."

Feeling like the walls were closing in on him, Garrett walked across the room and yanked the door open, pulling it closed behind him. Turning around, he rested his pounding forehead on the cool wall, tears burning his eyes.

Family drama wasn't his thing. It would all be so much easier with Jules by his side.

But she wasn't, so he'd just have to deal.

One weekend... One and a half days.

She'd spent thirty-six hours with the guy—give or take—and she was moping around like Eeyore on a very bad day.

Jules, standing on the balcony of her Montego Bay hotel, looked down at the poolside bar and noticed the staff replenishing the stock. She was due to give a cocktail demonstration in a little while, and she looked like roadkill. A flattened, dried-out husk of an opossum.

She needed to do her hair, slap on makeup, find her happy face and smile, dammit. But doing that on the beach yesterday almost killed her. She didn't know if she had the energy to give the hotel's guests what they wanted this afternoon. Or tonight.

Jules walked back into her hotel suite and placed her hands on the back of a sofa and lowered her head. She was in another exquisitely decorated suite in another foreign country, and next week, next month, she'd be somewhere else, doing the same thing.

This was what she wanted, she told herself, what she'd always wanted. To be free, untethered, able to dart across the world at a moment's notice. She didn't want a house, a family, a man tying her down, someone she had to consult before she made a decision.

She was *not* her mother... She would not dance to the beat of a man's drum.

But she missed Garrett. And she couldn't understand why as she'd spent so little time with him. But he got her, like no one else ever had, and she'd told him things that she'd kept buried for so long.

She trusted him, and she knew she could love him. And that's why she'd run. Because he made her feel too much, made her question her life, her beliefs, her lifelong plan.

If she spent a week with him, she'd be completely under his spell; a month with him and she'd not be able to make a decision without him.

No, it was better to be on her own. She'd get over this hump, this blip, and would be back to herself in a few days.

She hoped.

Hearing a knock on her door, Jules straightened, shaking out her fingers. She'd ordered a power smoothie from room service earlier—peanut butter, banana, milk and protein powder—in the hope that it would give her the lift she so desperately needed.

It couldn't hurt.

Jules walked into the hallway and yanked open the door, blinking when she saw two very unexpected faces. Then she blinked again.

Tinsley, dressed in a blueberry-colored sundress, dropped a kiss on her cheek and gave her a quick hug before Kinga nudged her aside to repeat her sister's action.

Okay, so this was *waaay* better than a power smoothie for a pick-me-up.

"What are you doing here?" she demanded, putting her hands to her cheeks.

Kinga pushed her hand into her ultrashort blond hair as they walked onto the balcony and into the warm air.

"Tinsley saw the video you posted yesterday and asked me what I thought about it. We both agreed it was terrible," Kinga said, dropping into a chair and putting her bare legs up onto the balcony railing. Like Tinsley, she wore a short sundress, but hers was a bright yellow. She looked like a worried sunbeam.

Jules rubbed her hand up and down her jaw. She knew she'd been a bit off yesterday, but she didn't think she'd been *that* bad.

Tinsley rubbed her shoulder before sitting down on the sofa. She patted the space next to her. "Relax, Ju. Kinga is being melodramatic."

Jules sat down, her gaze bouncing between her two friends.

"But it wasn't your best work," Tinsley continued. "You smiled and laughed and said everything you needed to…"

"But?"

"But your smile wasn't genuine, and your eyes were dull and sad," Kinga stated. "And because that's unusual for you, we commandeered a plane and headed south."

"Whose plane?" Jules asked. "Cody's or Griff's?"

Tinsley smiled. "Callum's."

"We figured if we were going to lose access to it

soon, we might as well get some use out of it," Kinga cheerfully added.

Jules frowned. "What are you talking about?"

"Ah, that's a long story, but right now, we want to find out what's going on with you," Tinsley said. "But we can't do this without a drink. I need a margarita."

Jules glanced at her watch. "I've got to work in an hour or so."

"We don't," Kinga said, climbing to her feet. She pointed her index finger at them. "I'll call room service and order. Don't start interrogating her until I get back, Tins."

When Kinga disappeared back into the suite, Jules looked at Tinsley. "How's Cody?"

Tinsley's smile bloomed, and happiness hit her startling blue eyes. "Lovely, thank you."

Tinsley's former brother-in-law was going to be her new husband, and Jules knew that she was finally with the right Gallant brother. "And your folks? And Callum?"

Tinsley rolled her eyes. "There's drama, lots of it. Callum has been moved to a private room and is being his normal, irascible self."

"Whatever happened about those DNA tests you took, the ones Callum gave you for Christmas?"

Tinsley shrugged. "God only knows. They were for a genealogical website so that we could trace the history of our DNA. Also, if anyone else has some of the same DNA, indicating a family tie of some sort, it flags it. But our tests haven't come back, and none of us are on the website. And that's weird because a friend of Cody's did his in the middle of February, and he got his results back within two weeks and was up on their website a day later."

"Weird."

"What's weird?" Kinga asked, dropping down into her seat.

"I was telling Ju about the delay in the DNA tests," Tinsley explained.

Kinga waved her words away. "On the scale of stuff to worry about, that is way down the list. We want to know what's upset you, Ju."

Jules turned her head to look at the beach and the azure waters of the Caribbean Sea. It was beautiful, but she'd far prefer to be at Kate's ranch, watching the snow fall on the Rockies. But with Garrett. Only with Garrett.

"Jules, talk to us," Tinsley implored.

She should. She needed to talk to someone. But where to start? With her childhood, with Kate losing her ranch, asking Garrett for help? The Valentine's Day Ball? Going to his office?

Did it matter? They were all tied up with each other.

Jules sighed and started to recount what had happened between her and Garrett. She spoke, interrupted only by the delivery of the margaritas. And then spoke some more while her friends simply listened.

When she finally wound down, Tinsley put her

hand on her knee and passed her a bowl-like glass. "Drink," she ordered her.

"I've got to work soon!" Jules protested.

"A sip, or even a half glass, won't hurt you," Tinsley insisted. Jules, seeing the determination in Tinsley's eyes, caved and sighed when the tart liquid hit her tongue. Lovely.

Kinga sat up, placed her heels on the edge of the chair and wrapped her arms around her shins. "Right, let me make sure I have the highlights. You bounced around the country, fleeing your abusive dad. You met Kate, who let you spend summers with her. Your dad found your mom in Denver and put her in the hospital, and he ended up dying in a car accident? Right so far?"

Jules nodded, appreciating Kinga's matter-of-fact voice.

"As a result, you vowed that you would never tie yourself to anyone or anything, ever? Not to a place or a man or a home?

"Kate is about to lose her ranch, so you asked Garrett Kaye—the man with a reputation for stripping companies, not rehabilitating them—to see if he could save Crazy Kate's? And you spent the weekend with him, and you slept with him?"

Tinsley picked up where Kinga left off. "And he asked to see you again, but you told him no, that you can't because you might fall in love with him and that's unacceptable?"

Jules nodded. Yeah, basically. She'd omitted the part about being, technically, a virgin, and how

Garrett cured her of her aversions to bedrooms. She glanced inside and wrinkled her nose. Well, that wasn't true. She'd only managed to sleep in a bedroom, in a bed, with him. She'd slept on couches, in her apartment, Cancun and here in Montego Bay, since leaving Colorado.

"You're in love with Garrett," Kinga stated, on a delighted hoot.

"I am *not* in love with him! I spent two days with him, not even that! People don't fall in love that quickly!"

"You did!" Kinga crowed.

"I did not!" Jules shot back, knowing she was lying. Of course she was in love with him, that arrogant, big, powerful, confident man. Dammit.

"Jules?" Tinsley softly asked.

She met Tinsley's sympathetic eyes and bit her lip, annoyed at the tears in her eyes. "I don't *want* to be in love with him. I don't want a man in my life, telling me what to do, how to act."

Tinsley and Kinga stared at her, their eyes wide with astonishment. They exchanged a long glance, and Tinsley put an arm around Jules's shoulder. "Baby girl, that's not fair."

Jules pulled away from Tinsley and moved into the corner of the couch, her body rigid with tension.

"No, don't get huffy, Jules," Tinsley said, in a clear but tough voice. "Look, we understand that you have some trust issues when it comes to guys. Who wouldn't when the first man who was supposed to love and protect you was a total bastard? But you know, you *know*, Garrett isn't like that!"

"I don't know that. How would I know that?" Jules demanded, her voice rising.

"Because you would never, ever have slept with him if you didn't trust him," Tinsley told her. "Your subconscious knows that he's a safe bet. That's why you were able to make love with him and fall asleep with him. You did fall asleep with him, right?"

Yeah, she had. With her head on his shoulder, her hand on his heart. She'd slept deeply, waking up feeling wonderful.

"Your head, your intellect, is just trying to protect you, but your heart knows that he would never physically hurt you," Kinga told her, sounding so very serious. "He's the guy for you, the first guy you've had sex with, the first guy you've fallen asleep with, the first guy you've trusted enough to let him share a bedroom with you. You've been waiting for him."

Jules stared at her, in total shock. "How did you know about me being a virgin, about not being able to sleep in a bedroom?"

Kinga sent her a smile full of love. "Remember that girls' weekend we spent in Vail, and you got so drunk on Dom Pedros and Irish coffees? You told us you were a virgin but not why. We've always wondered. As for not being able to sleep in a bedroom, on every trip we've taken, despite there being a bed for you, you've slept on couches, in hammocks, on decks. When you've stayed over at our places, despite us both having beautifully decorated guest suites, you've always slept on the couch. It's not rocket science, sweetie."

Well, shit. So much for thinking she had some secrets left.

Kinga dropped her legs and leaned forward, the fingers of her right hand playing with the enormous diamond on her left hand. "I never thought I'd find Griff, didn't think I needed love. But he makes my life better, in every way." She grinned and pulled a face. "Look, he annoys and frustrates me, and he calls me out, and I call him out. We're both strong-willed people, but it's an equal partnership, Jules."

"As is mine with Cody," Tinsley told her. "We think you could have the same type of relationship with Garrett, Ju."

"How do you know that?" Jules cried. "How do you know that, when I commit to him, he won't turn into a freak who'll try to control me?"

"Because if you look for them, there are signs that he respects women, Jules," Tinsley told her. "He's the son of a working single mom, and Emma would've slapped down any misogynistic ideas he had as a teenager. He doesn't have a gender pay gap at his company, and he has more women as managers in his organization than he does men. His exes only have good things to say about him, and his staff says he treats everyone the same—he's demanding but fair."

"And respectful of their time and appreciative of their efforts," Kinga explained.

"The point is, he might be tough and hard-assed, but he's a good guy," Tinsley added.

"Jules, what if you are wrong? What if you are making a choice based on fear? What if you miss out on the *one* guy who makes life a little brighter, more colorful, who rocks your world? In ten days or ten months or ten years, are you going to regret walking away from him?"

"But what if—" She couldn't complete the thought.

"What if it doesn't work out?" Kinga asked. "Then it doesn't work out. What if he's dominating? You call him on it, and if his behavior doesn't change, you walk. If he threatens you physically, you walk. If he hurts you, even if you just break a goddamn nail, we kill him," Kinga said, her tone matter-of-fact again. And Jules suspected she wasn't joking.

Tinsley gripped her hand in hers. "He won't hurt you, Jules, ever. Of that we are sure."

Jules saw the conviction in her friend's inky-blue eyes and moved her gaze to Kinga's. Kinga nodded her agreement, and Jules relaxed, just a fraction. She trusted her friends, trusted their intuition, far more than she trusted her own. If they believed she was safe, she would be. They would never encourage her to enter a situation that would cause her pain.

"We're not asking you to make a decision now, Ju," Tinsley told her, after draining her margarita glass. "We're just asking you to think about what we've said."

Kinga glanced at her watch. "You have a gig in twenty minutes, sweetie. While you're thinking, might I suggest a shower and a change of clothes? You look like hell."

Jules nodded. "I know. I do not want to go and throw bottles around and talk crap."

Honestly, she didn't know if doing pop-up bars, openings and celeb events was what she wanted to do at all anymore. She didn't know what she wanted to do, but darting around the world had lost its appeal. If she didn't have to support Kate and Peta, she'd pack it in tomorrow or, at the very least, take a long break. Actually, she did know what would make her heart sing... She wanted to see Garrett every day, go to bed with him, wake up with him, spend as much time as possible with him.

She stood up and wiped her sweaty hands on the seat of her denim shorts. "What if he tells me he's not interested?"

They smiled at her, bright, blinding smiles. "He won't," Kinga told her, oozing confidence. "But if you want to see him, check where he is first. He's been spending a lot of time in Colorado lately."

Colorado? Why on earth would he be there? The only link between him and Colorado was Crazy Kate's, so what was he up to? Was he buying out her assets, stripping her company?

There was only one way to find out, so Jules lunged for her phone and made an international call.

And later, when she made it to the beach and her temporary bar, her steps were lighter, and her eyes brighter.

She couldn't wait to return to Portland, to take a shot at the life she so desperately wanted.

Garrett straightened his silver tie and did up the button on his dark gray suit jacket. He stood by the bar and anxiously cast glances at the door to the restaurant, waiting for the arrival of the Ryder-Whites.

Earlier in the day, when James had called him to check his schedule for the next board meeting, his dad—God, he had a *dad*—told him Tinsley and Kinga were aware they had a brother and, before he could recover from that statement, invited him to join the family for a meal in the private dining room of Siena, one of Portland's best restaurants.

The entire family expected him to be present.

Garrett, supposedly the toughest, baddest ass in business, had butterflies in his stomach, and his mouth was as dry as ten-day-old bread.

He wanted to have a drink, take a Valium, hightail it out of the restaurant. What the hell did he know about being part of a family? God, he barely had a relationship with his mother.

"You look like a guy who needs a drink. Or a hug."

He slowly turned, and there she was, wearing a black-and-red plaid dress and thigh-high boots, the dress's asymmetrical hem showing off her thighs. Her hair hung down her back, and her smile, normally so bright, was turned down a notch.

"Uh..." He glanced at the door, expecting to look back and see that she'd disappeared.

But nope, Jules was still there and standing in

front of him, a long black coat over her arm. "What are you doing here?" he asked, his voice scratchy.

"Depending on how the next few minutes go, hopefully I'll be joining you for dinner," Jules told him. She looked around at the crowded bar and jam-packed restaurant. "Can we talk somewhere quiet? Maybe outside?"

She'd be an icicle in two seconds flat. Garrett shook his head and lifted his hand. Within ten seconds, a concierge materialized at his side. "If the Ryder-White family arrives, can you seat them at the bar? I will come and get them in due course."

"Certainly, sir."

Garrett locked his hand around Jules's wrist and led her down a small hallway, pushing open a frosted-glass door.

She walked inside, saw the flowers and the candles and the exquisitely set table and sighed. "It's perfect for a family dinner."

Family. He still wasn't used to the word. Garrett closed the door behind Jules and leaned against it, crossing his arms and trying to look casual. "You asked if we could talk. What's on your mind?"

Jules placed her coat over the back of the nearest chair, bent down to sniff a rose and showed him a good portion of her thigh. All that golden skin... His lungs held his breath, and his heart spluttered. How was he supposed to have a rational conversation when he was unable to think of anything but taking her to bed, making her his? Permanently.

"I hear you've acquired a family," Jules said, her

gaze inquisitive. Seeing his frown, she quickly continued. "Tinsley told me, on the understanding that I promised not to tell anyone. And I haven't."

"Yeah, it's a concept I am still wrapping my head around," Garrett replied.

"Well, they are thrilled. They've always wanted a big brother to torment."

She laughed at his expression, something he imagined to be somewhere between horror and...well, horror. "Relax, they'll go easy on you, for the first few days."

"Wonderful," Garrett dryly replied.

"If they ignore you, then you have a problem. If they tease and torment you, you're part of the family," Jules explained.

Right, that didn't make him feel any better.

"I'm thrilled for you, Garrett, and I'm thrilled for them. You need a family, and they need you."

He needed her, but he was damned if he was going to beg. Love wasn't love if it had to be coerced.

Jules played with the heavy silver bracelet on her arm, and when she finally looked up at him, he saw the sheen of tears in her eyes. "But that's not why I am here." She hauled in a deep breath and waved her hands in front of her eyes, as if trying to dry her tears before they fell. "I came to say thank you, for what you did for Kate. You saved their business and the ranch."

No, that was going too far. His guy just found an investment nobody thought to look for. "I didn't do anything, Ju. It was there, my guy noticed it and he did the heavy lifting."

"Your guy is amazing," Jules said, her eyes a deep gold. "You're amazing, and I can't thank you enough. What can I do, what can I say to show you how grateful I am?"

"Your goddamn gratitude is not what I want from you!"

His half shout surprised him, but Jules barely reacted. She just held his stormy eyes and slowly tipped her head to the side. "What do you want from me, Garrett?"

Why not just tell her? He was already miserable. If she walked out on him again, nothing would change. "I want you."

Her curious expression didn't change. "How do you want me? Exactly?"

It would be too easy to say *Up against the wall* or *Over the back of the couch*, but the time for hedging, fudging and playing word games was over. He wanted that. Of course he did—he'd never stop wanting her—but he wanted more. He wanted everything.

"I want you in my life, permanently. I want to wake up with you, play piano for you, ply you with decent coffee—"

She sighed. "I could do with one of your coffees right now."

He glared at her. "Really? That's what you went with?"

She waved her hand and pulled a face. "Sorry. I

didn't mean to interrupt. What else do you want from me?" she politely asked.

Oh, what the hell. He'd come this far, he might as well throw it all out there. "I want to be with you, have you be with me. But right now, the thing I want the most is your trust, the assurance that you know, deep down know, that I would never hurt you. Because if you can't give me that, nothing else matters," he added.

Jules saw the frustration in his eyes, the insecurity, the fear that she was, once again, going to turn him down. How brave he was! He was embracing a new family, getting to know his dad, wanting a relationship with his two willful sisters. And he'd just put himself out there, for her.

She felt humbled by his strength and his honesty.

"Before we get to that, I do just need to thank you, once again, from the bottom of my heart, for saving Kate's ranch. I will forever be grateful to you, and from now on, you will be treated like a god when we visit Kate and Peta."

Garrett waved her thanks away.

"You asked me if I trusted you, and I thought I didn't but...I do." Jules walked over to him and slid her hand under his suit jacket to find the spot above his heart. She picked up his hand and placed it on her chest, above her heart. "It was pointed out to me, by your sisters, that I would never have made love with you if I didn't. They also made me realize that you are the only person who has ever gotten me to sleep in a bedroom. I couldn't, not even at the ranch or when I was with them, do that. I haven't slept in a bedroom since I was a kid, but I did with *you*."

"Oh, baby."

Jules ignored the slow slide of tears running down her cheeks. "Only you, Garrett. That's how much I trust you. I also love you, by the way," she added, lifting her shoulder. "So much."

Garrett's big hands clasped her face, and he used his thumbs to wipe away her tears. He placed his forehead against hers and dropped a hard kiss on her mouth before abruptly pulling back. "If I kiss you, I won't stop. I've missed you so much, Juliana."

"I missed you, too," Jules said on a tiny hiccup. "I dropped two bottles of tequila and a bottle of Cointreau because I couldn't concentrate. My mind was too full of you."

Garrett placed his thumb in the center of her bottom lip. "How much time do we have together before you have to fly off again?"

"How much time can you spare me? I asked my agent to cancel my bookings for the foreseeable future. She squawked and squealed, but I'm currently unemployed."

"Why did you do that?" Garrett asked.

Jules held his wrists, her eyes tracing his beloved face. "I wanted to give this, our relationship, a little time to settle, for us to get to know each other better." She saw the satisfaction in his eyes and smiled.

"Now that I know that I don't have to support Kate and Peta, I can rethink my career. I'm tired, a little burned-out, so sick of sleeping on hotel-room couches. I want to be with you, but I also want to see what else I can do, be. Maybe write a cocktail book, a travel memoir. I'll get back on the road at some point, sometime, but I don't ever want to go back to the frenetic pace I was working before."

"Tell me where you need to be, how you want to do it, and I'll rearrange my schedule to be with you."

"You'd do that for me?" she asked, shocked at his generous offer.

"I'd do anything for you, Ju. This is a partnership. We have to be able to compromise. I can work remotely. I do it all the time. My career doesn't take preference over yours, ever. We sink or swim together."

Jules stood on her tiptoes to brush her mouth against his. "Does that mean you love me?" she asked, her heart bouncing off her ribs.

"Oh, Jules, how can you doubt that? I love you with everything I have, everything I am. My world doesn't make sense without you. Be with me. Be mine."

Jules clasped the back of his neck. "Always."

And when he kissed her, Jules could taste the love on his lips, feel it in the big hands that held her, in the body that he'd placed between her and the world. He'd love and protect her, cherish her. Of that she had no doubt.

She was home, and he now owned her heart.

Jules sighed when he deepened their kiss, and desire flashed, hot and fast, through her. She groaned into his mouth and smiled as he bent his knees to wrap his arm behind her thighs to lift her. She fumbled for the button to open his suit jacket, found it and slid her legs around his waist, desperate to get close to him.

Their kiss burned hotter, more desperate, and Garrett placed his hands under her dress, kneading her butt cheeks. She needed him. Now.

From a place far, far away, Jules heard the door open and the trill of feminine laughter. Pulling her mouth off Garrett's, she peeked over his shoulder to see his sisters, doubled over with mirth.

She tried to shoo them away, but they just shook their heads. Kinga, the brat, in a singsong voice, was the first to speak. "*Da-ad*, Garrett has his hand up Ju's dress."

Garrett groaned, and Jules grinned as she slid down his big body. "And so it starts," she told him. "Strap in for a hell of a ride, Kaye."

He grinned at her. "As long as I have you at my side, I'm good." He kissed her before turning around to nail his sisters with a mock-hard look. "I told the concierge to ask you to wait. Do you ever listen?"

Kinga and Tinsley strolled over to them, and both of them kissed Garrett's cheek. "No, we never do. We do what we want, when we want."

Griff O'Hare looked at Cody, and they both nodded. "We can vouch for that. We blame James."

James grinned at them, his arm around Penelope's waist. "There were days when we were convinced they'd be the leaders of a prison gang."

"Funny," Tinsley muttered, scowling at her father.

"You're just excited to have another male in the family to dilute the estrogen," Kinga informed James.

"What are we, fairy dust?" Griff protested, his hands on his hips, scowling at Kinga.

"Play nicely, children," Penelope said, walking up to Garrett. "Welcome to the madness, Garrett. I hope you have a spine of steel."

Jules grinned at Garrett. "Having second thoughts about your ready-made family, darling?"

He looked at his sisters, then at his father, and smiled. "A thousand and one, but I'll deal. Once I commit, I stick." He bent his head and kissed her, and Jules knew that it was a promise he'd never break.

To his family and to her.

* * * * *

Who owns the missing Ryder International shares?
And what decades-old secret is Penelope hiding?

*On his birthday, London-based author
Sutton Marchant discovers he's heir to a massive
fortune, but only if he spends two months at
The Rossi Inn and attends the famous
Ryder International Charity Ball.*

*Innkeeper Lowrie Lewis is ecstatic when the
famous author books the entire inn to
maintain his privacy.*

*But Lowrie doesn't like secrets and it's
obvious that Sutton has a few...*

*Don't miss the final story in the
Dynasties: DNA Dilemma series*
The Secret Heir Returns

COMING NEXT MONTH FROM

⊕ HARLEQUIN
DESIRE

#2875 BOYFRIEND LESSONS
Texas Cattleman's Club: Ranchers and Rivals
by Sophia Singh Sasson
Ready to break out of her shell, shy heiress Caitlyn Lattimore needs
the help of handsome businessman Dev Mallik to sharpen her dating
skills. Soon, fake dates lead to steamy nights. But can this burgeoning
relationship survive their complicated histories?

#2876 THE SECRET HEIR RETURNS
Dynasties: DNA Dilemma • by Joss Wood
Secret heir Sutton Marchant has no desire to connect with his birth
family or anyone else. But when he travels to accept his inheritance, he
can't ignore his attraction to innkeeper Lowrie Lewis. Can he put the
past behind him to secure his future?

#2877 ROCKY MOUNTAIN RIVALS
Return to Catamount • by Joanne Rock
Fleur Barclay, his brother's ex, should be off-limits to successful rancher
Drake Alexander, especially since they've always despised one another.
But when Fleur arrives back in their hometown, there's a spark neither
can ignore, no matter how much they try...

#2878 A GAME BETWEEN FRIENDS
Locketts of Tuxedo Park • by Yahrah St. John
After learning he'll never play again, football star Xavier Lockett finds
solace in the arms of singer Porscha Childs, until a misunderstanding
tears them apart. When they meet again, the heat is still there. But they
might lose each other once more if they can't resolve their mistakes...

#2879 MILLION-DOLLAR CONSEQUENCES
The Dunn Brothers • by Jessica Lemmon
Actor Isaac Dunn needs a date to avoid scandal, and his agent's sister,
Meghan Squire, is perfect. But pretending leads to one real night...
and a baby on the way. Will this convenient arrangement withstand the
consequences—and the sparks—between them?

#2880 CORNER OFFICE CONFESSIONS
The Kane Heirs • by Cynthia St. Aubin
To oust his twin brother from the family company, CEO Samuel Kane
sets him up to break the company's cardinal rule—no workplace
relationships. But it's *Samuel* who finds himself tempted when
Arlie Banks awakes a passion that could cost him everything...

YOU CAN FIND MORE INFORMATION ON UPCOMING HARLEQUIN TITLES,
FREE EXCERPTS AND MORE AT HARLEQUIN.COM.

HDCNM0422

Maxton eyed Teagan and asked, "Isn't there something I
didn't get to see?"

She smiled. "If you mean my bedroom, you gotta earn
it, playboy."

"Sounds like a challenge," he quipped.

She shook her head. "No. More of a requirement."

He laughed, then gently dragged the tip of his index
finger along her jawline. "You're going to make me work
for this. I just know it."

Her answer was a sultry smile. "We'll just have to see
what happens."

"Truth is, I really don't have the time for a relationship
right now."

If she took offense at his statement, she didn't show it.
"Neither do I."

"So, what are we doing here?"

She shrugged. "A fling? A dalliance? I don't think it really matters what we call it, so long as we both understand what it is…and what it isn't."

Their gazes met and held, and the sparkle of mischief in her eyes threatened to do him in. "Enlighten me, Teagan. What will we be doing, exactly?"

"We hang out…have a little fun. No strings, no commitments. And, above all, we don't let this thing interfere with our work or our lives." She pressed her open palm against his chest. "That is, if you think you can handle it."

"Seems reasonable." *I like this approach. Seems like we're on one accord.*

Her smile deepened. "Tomorrow is my only other free day for a while. Why don't you meet me at the Creamery, right near Piedmont Park? Say around seven?"

"I'll be there." He wanted to kiss her but couldn't read her thoughts on the matter. So he grazed his fingertip over her soft glossy lips instead.

"See you then," she whispered.

Satisfied, he opened the front door and stepped out into the afternoon sunshine.

Don't miss what happens next in…
After Hours Temptation
by Kianna Alexander.

Available June 2022 wherever
Harlequin Desire books and ebooks are sold.

Harlequin.com